Versions of Life

A Collection Of Short Stories

NEAL LANDER

authorHOUSE®

AuthorHouse™
1663 Liberty Drive
Bloomington, IN 47403
www.authorhouse.com
Phone: 833-262-8899

Published by AuthorHouse 01/21/2021

ISBN: 978-1-6655-1477-4 (sc)
ISBN: 978-1-6655-1476-7 (e)

Library of Congress Control Number: 2021901303

Print information available on the last page.

I am not what I would consider a "religious" type of person. I do believe in God and Jesus Christ, but I'm no bible thumper by any means. I live in Dayton, Ohio and this small city is crazy sometimes. There is a violent under current here that appears at different and unexpected times. Life it seems has very little value nowadays. There are weeks in which someone is killed almost every day. Many of my classmates and people I grew up with have been killed senselessly. As soon as all of the General Motors and Chrysler jobs dried up and the crack cocaine replaced them, my poor city suffered mightily. I look back and wonder sometimes why I was spared death at a young age. Only to have my heart, my life, my sanity torn to pieces. I was pretty much raised in the church. My Granny had me go to church with her regularly. I was very close with my Grandmother. My Granny was my heart and she shared much of her wisdom with me regularly. My beliefs about religion come directly from her teachings. I remember complaining about not having enough money and she looked me in the eye and told me "It's not always about how much money you make Alan, but what you do with the money you make". I miss our talks and time together. One of the many things she instilled in me was that "we must stay strong in Christ to keep them demons up off of us. We either fight against the demons or we become demons ourselves." she would say. I never really understood what she meant back then. One thing for sure is that I knew that I didn't want them demons on me. She made it sound like having demons on you was the worst thing that could ever happen to a person.

I witnessed a demon first hand while with my Granny one afternoon. My cousin was married to this guy whom I considered a loser. She was always mistreating the young man. She beat on him publicly both physically and vocally. He would never so much as raise his voice to her in response to the foul treatment. That's the reason that I considered him a loser. I just couldn't fathom why he accepted such maltreatment from her. When he wasn't around my Granny would berate her about how she treated her husband. She would not listen though. Well sadly she had gotten herself a boyfriend to go along with her husband. Only she never told her husband about her boyfriend, and she never told her boyfriend about her husband. Well I'm sure that you can see where this is going. When her husband found out about the boyfriend all of his timid ways went out the window. When he showed up at my Granny's door something was different about him. He was always quiet, but the look in his eye was chilling. He asked us if we had seen his wife that day? Neither of us had seen her. My Granny asked him if he was alright. He shook his head yes and turned to leave. After he was gone my Granny said "There's a demon on that boy Alan". Later that evening he caught up with his wife and her boyfriend and he attacked them both with a machete. After he finished hacking their lifeless bodies he sat down and cried until the police arrived and took him away. I knew right then and there that I did not want them demons on me for sure. Geez!

My Granny was strong and resolute in her beliefs, and she did not accept any mistreatment of me or any of her grandchildren. One Sunday after church they were serving dinner plates, so Granny and I grabbed us a table. After we were situated, I went to get our plates. My Granny was using a walker at this time so I did most of the running for her. One of the ladies serving the food acted like I was being greedy because I had two plates, so she stopped me and proceeded to scold me. She pissed me off so bad that I couldn't speak. Any words that would have come out of my mouth would have been very disrespectful, so I remained quiet. I filled my Grannies plate and went back to our table. When I sat down, she asked me where my plate was at? Before I could even respond she was up on her walker headed to the food line. I don't know what my Granny said to that lady, but the lady came over to our table carrying two more plates. "Why didn't you tell me that you were with Granny?"

she asked me with a fake ass smile. I just looked away from her because even though that lady was wrong and acting fake my Granny taught us to respect our elders no matter how ignorant they may be. Years later after my beloved Granny had passed on, I discovered exactly what she was trying to get me to understand. I found out what those demons were, and I found out that they were on me.

I'm getting ahead of myself please allow me to tell you a few things about my life before I discovered the demons. I'm Alan Pierce and I was happily married to my beautiful wife Melody. I worked two jobs almost daily. Home improvement and repair during the day and I also did janitorial work in the evenings. I worked hard to help take care of my wife and our two children. In the mornings after taking the kids to school I would eat breakfast and then go to work on some houses. I was a general contractor or handyman if you will. I had built up a good reputation and clientele because I was honest and hard working. My schedule changed from day to day depending on what type of calls I received. Some days would be slow, and I would maybe replace a water heater or faucet. Some days would be hectic and busy filled with furnace work or complete pipe replacement or just running around all day doing odd jobs. I also had a janitorial business that I attended to in the evenings. My contracts consisted of six properties, four day-care facilities, a manufacturing plant, and a doctor's office. It was relatively easy work. I emptied the trash, cleaned the bathrooms and dusted and mopped the floors. My day would start at 7am and end usually around 10pm. I worked hard as hell, but it was cool. I loved my work and I loved my life. I was the happiest I had ever been.

My wife Melody was great. She kept our home clean, and she kept the children fed and bathed. We were the perfect team in my mind because she maintained our household perfectly and I made sure that our bills were paid. If it would have become necessary for her to get a job it would have been cool. Shit we do what we gotta do to survive and I never had any hang-ups about a woman's place. In my mind a man and a woman are a team. We take care of each other no matter what. Her not working a job at the time was preferred though because it meant that our children never had to go to daycare. And even after our kids were school age, Mel continued to be the best housewife. We had two children almost exactly one year apart. The eldest, my daughter Shannon's birthday is on May 7th, and my son Chris's day is on May 1st. It wasn't on purpose that they came back to back like that, but it worked out. Melody was so good with our children. She taught them good manners and was stern on them when it came to school and chores, but she also played around with them a lot. A stranger observing their interaction would smile at the open display of love and affection they showed each other. Sometimes I would feel a tinge of jealousy at their relationship because I didn't have that closeness with my babies. I rationalized my guilt with how much I worked so my kids would never have to do without like I did growing up. To make up for the time I would spoil them with gifts all year around. Not just on holidays or birthdays. But it never made up for the time, and I regret not spending more time with my babies while I had the chance.

Shannon my eldest acted like a miniature Melody. She mimicked her mom to a fault, I thought that it was the cutest thing. She was an excellent student and I was very proud of her. She was just so responsible to be 12 years old. When I was 12 all I thought about was playing ball, running in the woods, or making bugs fight. Well they say girls are more mature than boys growing up and I can honestly see that in Shannon my little lady. We never had to tell Shannon to clean her room, or do her homework, she just did it all on her own. After school activities were not high on her list although she did like soccer. She always reminded us of her practice times and games. Like I said very responsible. Chris on the other hand reminded me so much of myself at that age. At age 11 he didn't have a care in the world. He was very active in all aspects of his young life. He enjoyed playing any sport, and any game. Once Chris got started it was hard to get him to stop. He was like the battery bunny he just kept going and going and going.

Thinking back to my childhood many of the lessons that I was taught have always remained with me. Proper education was preached in my parent's home while I was growing up, but getting a job was also a part of my reality. The miscellaneous kiddy things that I wanted like video games or toys were bought with my hustle money. My mom and dad worked hard but we were very poor because the jobs they had didn't pay very well at all. I still was happy growing up. I thought we were a middle-class family until I got older and gained an understanding of economics and social standards. Even as young as 7 and 8 years old I worked. I honestly cannot remember a time in my life when I wasn't working, hustling, trying to make a dollar. There was an older couple for whom I did work for that were as poor as we were. They paid me with homemade fudge. That fudge was absolutely delightful. I miss them and that wonderful fudge to this day. I also carried newspapers, I cut grass, I shoveled snow, I basically scoured our neighborhood hustling. Even so I never felt like we were poor. Our lights never got turned off. We always had food. We always had running water and clean clothes. I say all of that because I had friends that were going through some or all those dilemmas. My granny always told me that we were blessed, and I believed her.

Growing up was annoying at times because for some reason or another I attracted bullies and assholes who fucked with me. I tried; I honestly tried to be peaceful and calm through it all. For the most part I was successful at ignoring when people tried to pick on me, but there were a few instances where I embarrassed myself and my parents. I share these episodes for the sake of clarity, please bear with me. One episode occurred after we had recently moved into a new neighborhood. I was riding my bike minding my business when a group of 6 or 7 boys approached me and pushed me off my bike. I fell and skinned my knee up pretty good. Needless to say, I was irate, but the anger was multiplied when one of the boys yelled at me "Can you see motherfucker?! You tryna run me and my boys over?!" Instead of a vocal reply he received punches to his face and upper body in response to his asinine statement. The crowd that had developed out of nowhere broke us up. One of his friends threw him a stick and he swung it at me barely missing me. I took off running up the alleyway with him chasing behind yelling and laughing. He thought I was running to get away, but I was looking for my own stick. I saw a branch that was handy, so I grabbed it quickly and turned on him and commenced to beat him in his head with the branch. One of the spiny limbs of the branch stuck in his head and he screamed as he ran away bleeding from his injury.

After he ran off screaming, I came to my senses. It was like I was asleep and dreaming at the same time. It was a very eerie feeling. I picked up my bike and walked home with all of the kids watching me strangely. His mother had the nerve to walk him to our door and show my mom what I had done to him. He had required several stitches in his head. I have to give my mom credit because she calmly listened to the woman's story before replying "Your son must have done something to Alan because he's a very peaceful and quiet boy" she told his mom calmly before calling me to the door. "Alan!" she yelled even though I was listening to the whole situation out of eye shot. "Yes ma'am?" I responded politely as I approached the doorway. "What happened between you and this boy today?" she asked sternly. I looked at him with his bandaged head and sad face and it was all I could do not to laugh at the asshole. "When I was riding my bike him and his friends pushed me off my bike and I hurt my leg" I paused to show my scraped-up knee before continuing. "He picked up a stick and tried to bully me so I found my own stick and got him before he could get me" I continued excitedly. "Mama him and his friends started with me. I was minding my own business" I continued sheepishly. My mom then turned to the woman and stated with conviction "I told you my boy is peaceful, but I raise him not to let anybody bully him. Teach your boy not to be a bully and he won't need stitches" she continued with the attitude and tone that only a mother standing up for her child can muster. I was so proud of my mom.

The overwhelming pride surging through my chest was cut short just as soon as the boy and his mom left our door. "What the hell you doing busting that boys head open?" she yelled at me. "Mama he started it" I stammered meekly. She continued to deride me until my father got home. "Alan done bust some little nigga head and his mom talking about suing us" she told my father. By this time, I just knew I was gonna catch a beat down because my dad did not fuck around at all. Hell, for the most part my mom did the discipline because she thought my dad was too rough on the ass whippings. That bitch threatening to sue us was what made her tell my dad. My dad listened to the whole story and then told me to come with him to the garage. The garage was my dad's sanctuary, and he only called you to the sanctuary if you were about to catch a serious beat down. I resigned myself to this ass whipping even though in my mind I truly felt like I didn't deserve it. When we got to the garage my dad shut the door and told me to sit down. "Alan I am proud that you stood up for yourself" he began solemnly. "Don't ever let a motherfucker think that he can bully you" he continued with conviction. Then he told me to go to bed.

Throughout my childhood there were many instances of unexpected violence and craziness. One episode occurred where I didn't use any physical violence, and I didn't receive a positive reaction from my dad either. We were living in an apartment complex with a pool one winter. The pool was not drained in the winter so it would freeze over and we could skate and slide on the frozen surface. It was me and my sister and our little friend Danny. I say little because Danny was smaller than both me and my sister. A couple moved into our complex and they had a daughter. That girl was huge. She immediately called herself bullying us. I really did not pay her any mind until she put her hands on Danny. He ran home crying and she turned on my sister and I "What you wanna do?" she yelled at us. We both ignored her at that moment, but messing with my friend Danny was a no no. That night I had a dream of her big ass drowning in the pool. The next day I plotted with Danny and my sister on how we were going to make the big bitch pay. So we waited for her to come outside and we commenced to yelling profanities at her. She gave chase. We ran across the pool and all of us being light weight and little it was nothing, but when her big ass tried to chase us, she fell through the ice. We laughed as she cried for help. An apartment maintenance man had witnessed the entire scene and he ran over to get her out of the frigid water. My dad told me that she could have died and that was why I got my ass beat. She never tried to bully any of us again, hell she didn't even speak to any of us again. That ass beating was well worth it.

Like I said before assholes and bullies were attracted to me like bears to honey. When I was in middle school there was a group of 3 boys that chose me to fuck with daily. Finally, after weeks of enduring the constant beratement I caught one of them at the park by himself and kicked his ass. For some reason I thought that that would make them leave me alone. The next day they jumped me. We all lived in the same hood, so I went looking and found another one of them alone. I kicked his ass even worse than the other guy. The next day they jumped me again. That night I dreamed of playing in a baseball game, but I just kept striking out. I was just swinging the bat, swinging the bat, swinging the bat. Now them jumping me was bad and it was cowardly but honestly it really didn't harm me. It was the principality of the situation that made me take my aluminum bat and try to cripple each one of them. The cops came to my house to question me about the situation. I denied it all of course and there was no proof. Only their word against mine. It was well documented the bully behavior these boys exhibited on a daily basis. On the other hand, I was a good student, a quiet, well behaved student. No charges were ever filed but after the cops left my dad questioned me about it. I described the treatment the boys had been giving me to my dad and I explained that I couldn't remember precisely what happened with the bat. It was all very blurry in my mind and I could not explain it. Through it all the one common theme was that I would blackout during those episodes of violence. I had trouble remembering the events. Almost like it never happened. As I grew older the episodes of violence stopped altogether, and I went out of my way to avoid any chance of conflict. I grew to truly despise physical or verbal altercations.

Once I became a grown ass man the only thing that I cared about was my family. My little family and I went to church on occasion and I rationalized that because I worked almost every day that we were excused from church service. Since I worked for myself, I couldn't afford to turn down any jobs because we needed the money. At least that's the excuse that I pounded into my brain. As I look back now maybe that was what let the demons in. Maybe I should have been taking my family to church like my Granny did me. I should have been giving God his time especially since I was so blessed. I wonder if I could have prevented the heart ache and hard times headed our way. Excuses are just like buttholes. Everybody has one and they stink. So as much as I harp on work and jobs, I should have taken the time out for my family. I should have always made time for the Lord my father. I should have led my family down the paths of righteousness instead of leading us straight into the black pits of hell. As the saying goes "hindsight is 20/20". I refer to those hellish days as "the demon's time". Now that the demon's time has ended; at least for now, my life has been forever changed and I still cry frequently.

The demon's time began soon after Melody's mother died unexpectedly. They were very close, and she took it hard. We all took it hard because her mom was a real sweetheart. Life has a way of bringing us all to the brink at one time or another. This was one of those times except it pushed us over the brink and into the abyss. I did what I could to console her, but she was unreachable. I believe Mel felt guilty about her mom's death even though it wasn't her fault. She perhaps regretted the time that she let get away. Believing that she still had time to do all the things that she wanted to do and to say all of the things that she wanted to say to her mom. It's crazy how so many of us take for granted our time here on earth. Procrastination tricking us into believing that we have tomorrow or the next day to do what we should be doing now. I could relate to what she was feeling because I felt crushed when my granny passed away. I regretted not spending more time with her, and I regretted not visiting her more when she went to hospice. It was just so hard to see my granny like that, because she had always been so strong and beautiful. To watch her when she was sickly and dying was just too much for me to bear. Looking back now I realize just how selfish I was and it saddens me. We all have our own way of dealing with pain and sorrow and I don't want to sound like I'm judging how Mel dealt with her pain and sorrow. However, it was extremely tough on our little family.

After the funeral I thought that she would start to get better and accept that death is a part of life. But Melody continued to get worse, she neglected her appearance and hygiene. Looking back now I realize that the demons were on my poor Mel. She had become so distant to me and the kids. And when she wasn't being distant, she was downright mean as hell. Spending hours in the bathroom each day. It was like she was sleep walking through each day. The children attempted to alert me to our predicament, but I was either in denial or exhausted from my work schedule. Either way I did nothing to change her or our course. I'm not sure I could have done anything at that point because the demon or demons were on poor Mel. The kids were so sad each day. I failed my babies. They deserved so much better than what I provided. How could I have been so blind? Lord please reverse time. Please take us back to before the demons came. I promise to do better, and not miss any Sundays. Shannon cornered me and explained to me that something was very wrong with her mom, and she wanted me to fix it. "Dad you're always fixing on something, well we need you to fix mom right now" she yelled at me. "Ok baby I hear you. I will fix this" I replied solemnly.

I started paying close attention to everything Mel did now. I asked her why she spent so much time in the bathroom and she told me that she was sick and in pain and that I needed to mind my own business. "You are my business" I yelled back at her. She started going to the doctor and receiving pain and depression meds. I absolutely despised when she was on those pills. Melody was like a zombie when she was on those damn pills. Every day she drifted further away from us. Soon the meds she got from prescriptions just wasn't enough, so she would buy them off the streets. This practice was very expensive. Pills cost anywhere from 7.00 for each pill up to 12.00 depending on whom we purchased them from. And Mel was taking anywhere from six to ten pills daily. I know that I was enabling Mel, but I could not bear to see her in pain and hurting the way she was. Believe me if I could turn back the hands of time I would do so in a heartbeat. My enabling Mel was the worst thing that I could have done. Not long after that I discovered that she had been snorting heroin. She explained to me that it was cheaper than the pills. Stupid me believed that somehow, we would come out of this and have our normal lives back. I underestimated the power of drugs and the demons that accompany those drugs. I suppose since I have never been on any drugs besides weed and alcohol, I will never understand the appeal of what I consider to be hard drugs. The heroin had my wife and had begun the destruction of our lives. She never slept in the bed with me anymore. She would be in the bathroom or on the couch nodding off.

I called myself taking charge of the situation and I put her in rehab. It was a six-week course that was supposed to bring Mel back to us. For a time, things smoothed out somewhat, but my baby just wasn't the same. Her smile was sad, her eyes were not shining like they once did, she didn't take the same pride in her appearance that she used to. After that attempt at rehab she was a little better. A little bit of her old self shined through. That lasted about two weeks after she came home, then things began to get worse day by day. Things started to walk out of our house. The kids video games, money, anything of any value. Then she graduated to shop lifting because our valuable things were gone, or we hid them from her. She became very adept at stealing and was fearless. I came home to various electronics in our home that I didn't buy. Clothes were her specialty because she would have bags upon bags of clothing. She called it "shopping" and she shopped almost every day. All the little things I had become accustomed to such as delicious aromas of dinner cooking when I came home from work, back rubs, feet massages, and sex were non-existent. I barely even saw my wife then. Shopping and drugs dominated her every waking moment. We argued almost daily, and I felt completely helpless. As much as I wanted to fix this I was completely out of my league when it came to demons and drugs.

My children were sad and began to act out in school. I had to take time off of work to deal with my children. We would talk, and we would cry. Somehow, they believed that their mom's condition was their fault. Chris would ask if he could do anything to help his mommy and all I could do was close my eyes and pray. Shannon was quiet and subdued; she was trying to hold her pain in and keep it to herself. I explained to them that their mom was very sick but that she would get better. My naïve beliefs were very much out of touch. My biggest shame from all of the craziness is that I had failed to protect my babies. I had failed as a father and as a man. Each day I would contemplate and invite death to take me. There was nothing to comfort me, no solace from the pain I felt, I use to wish that I could just feel nothing ever again. I soon started to have blackouts pretty regularly. I supposed that it was a way for me to cope with the disparity that ruled my life. I no longer could deal with confrontation or adversity. My mind would shelter me from the harsh reality of my desolate life, and even though I prayed for death at the time the Lord my God would not take me. I must pay for my stupidity, and my failure, and that payment is living each day while not really living each day at all.

One night I awoke to voices in the living room. It was after 3am so I'm very curious and annoyed at the same time. As I made my way into the living room the voices stopped. My wife was there alone. "Who were you talking to?" I asked her looking around the room. "No one" she replied. I know damn well I heard you talking to someone and it was a man's voice. Where is he hiding? "I was talking to myself" she stammered. By now I was very angry, and I was looking around the room for hiding places. There were no hiding places. After a few moments I sat down confused and disoriented. I know what I heard. "What's going on Mel?" I asked. "How can we fix this? What can I do?" I continued. Mel just sat there staring blankly ahead as if in deep thought. Finally, she said "baby take the kids and leave me, I'm just slowly killing us all". Weeks later I would discover that she was talking to a demon. The next several days were a blur. I can hardly remember anything from that time. I dreamed that I had hunted a man and shot him several times before stabbing him several times. The dream was very realistic and vivid. "I must be losing my mind" I thought to myself.

I pushed her into trying rehab again, and she reluctantly agreed. This program was an in-patient six-month ordeal. They were supposed to teach her coping skills to deal with her depression as an alternative to drugs. After two weeks her counselor asked me to have a private conference with him about my wife. I didn't know what to expect from this man, but nothing could have prepared me for what he told me. He explained to me how things were going and asked me if she had any history of mental illness. Apparently, she had been talking to herself with dual personalities he says. "What does that mean sir?" I asked. He explained that she was talking to herself with her normal voice and a man's voice. An evil gravelly voice. "I couldn't believe that it was coming from her" he said. I thought back to the night in our living room and a chill ran down my spine. That same voice is what I heard that night. The counselor told me that I should take her to a mental health facility that would be better equipped and prepared to handle our situation. He recommended a place called Groves mental health facility. I reached out to them and received an appointment.

I blacked out once again and for the next several days everything was a blur. It seemed like my mind was floating in some murky middle ground between reality and a very dark place for which I have no name. I dreamed that I was hunting demons this time. Several demons. I was like a ninja tracking and killing demons before they were even aware that I was hunting them. These fantasies were an escape from my sad reality I rationalized. And I relished the time away from reality even if it did involve dark, strange, and unbelievable dreams about murder. I could remember all the people who treated me unfairly. I placed their likeness on the demons that I killed in my dreams. It made me feel good to get revenge on those vile, evil people, even if it was only in my imagination. One morning I awoke on the kitchen floor with bloody mud covering me from head to toe. I was so frightened that my entire body began to shake uncontrollably. I began to ask myself what the hell was going on. I began to wonder if I was in fact losing my mind. Whose blood was I covered in? Where had I been? Why couldn't I remember? I got naked and looked for any injuries that I might have sustained but I found nothing. Not even a scratch anywhere on my body. Maybe Mel wasn't the only one of us that needed mental help. My children must have noticed a difference in me as well because they started to avoid me like I had the plague. They spent most of the time with my sister Yvonne these days. I was in a constant fog and unable to care for my babies. Thank goodness for my sweet sister.

Groves mental health facility was state of the art. I was impressed with the place. The grounds were immaculate, the staff were courteous, and very professional. The doctor who would handle our case was an exceptionally beautiful woman. Doctor Madeline Turley was her name. To be completely honest the doctor was so beautiful that I found myself feeling uncomfortable around her because I felt like I was staring at her or ogling her. I felt guilty like I was cheating on my wife even though I had just met this woman. This was a very unsettling feeling. The good doctor seemed oblivious to my predicament because she just carried on with her introductions and credentials. After we talked for a while about the situation concerning Mel, and I explained everything we had been going through, Doctor Turley explained her plan for treatment. I wondered if I should have informed the doctor of my blackouts. I felt nervous about telling anyone about my obvious mental instability. I had to remain strong for my family and any signs of weakness could not be tolerated. I felt like me having blackouts was a sign of weakness. Like I couldn't deal with the reality of my life so I would blackout like a little weakling. That was unacceptable. My blackouts were my problem and my secret. Let's listen to the good doctor's treatment plan for my wife, and forget all about those thoughts that had flashed across my mind.

First, they would observe her while she slept and during her waking hours to see if there are any observable signs or triggers associated with the voices. I was encouraged with the pretty doctor's plan; however, Mel wasn't encouraged at all. Melody was being very difficult about the whole situation. After we had Melody admitted and checked into her room, I tried to cheer her up. Her attitude was very frankly pissing me off. I was going thru hell dealing with this bullshit and she had the audacity to have an attitude? I was trying my best to be patient with all of this, but my patience was wearing thin at this point. After a time, we sat back down with Doctor Turley. The good doctor perhaps could sense the tension between us, because she tried to make small talk complimenting Mel's appearance. The attempt at small talk was futile because Mel was acting out. After about ten minutes of dealing with her attitude I angrily asked her what her freaking problem was. She ignored me and went to her room and closed the door. Doctor Turley and I sat there in awkward silence for a moment before I decided to leave and go home.

The next day I received a call from Doctor Turley explaining to me how the evening and night had gone. She informed me that at about 2am Mel had begun to talk with those voices and that they had recorded them. She asked if I would like to hear the recording. Of course, I did want to hear it, so we scheduled a time two days in the future. The days passed and I met with Doctor Turley to listen to the recordings and get an assessment of Mel's condition. It was rather alarming to hear Mel talking to what sounded like a ghoul. I asked the doctor was there any way that someone else could have been present in the room with Mel. She explained to me that that was quite impossible. "Mel was locked in her room alone from 9pm until 6am" she continued. She explained that all the patients must be locked in their rooms each night. "We used to allow much more freedom here Mr. Pierce, however that just doesn't work well with drug rehab programs" she stated flatly. "We had so many patients run away from the facility mostly at night that we changed our policies and treatment approach" she continued. "I believe we can successfully defeat your wife's condition" said Doctor Turley with confidence.

I was very grateful for the offer of help, but I was not at all confident in our ability to combat this evil. Doctor Turley spoke as though this was any other medical dilemma with a logical solution. "Doctor Turley how can we expect to deal with this?" I asked. She calmly explained that science can answer any and, all queries. The more she talked the more comforted I became. Soon I was encouraged that we could and would fix this. To calm the situation doctor Turley told me that the children and I should have a break from Melody and her malady. "Sir your children are in shock and so are you. You should take them away for a week or so. After that let's see where things stand". She wanted us to give her treatment plan a chance without us being a distraction. I was taken aback by the doctor's statement and somewhat offended. "Doctor we are her family, not a distraction" I stated. "Mr. Pierce, I meant no offense" she said. "Trust me and trust the process please" she continued. Her smile put me at ease, so I agreed. Maybe the doctor was right. Maybe we did need a break from all of this.

Reluctantly the children and I took a trip to Colorado to visit with family, some of which we hadn't seen in years. I must admit I was very relaxed and at ease. I hadn't felt that good in some time. Since the demon time had started my head was always cloudy and my mood was a constant melancholy. I looked at my kids and I could tell that they were feeling better also. I couldn't remember the last time I had seen them smiling and playing around with one another. I smiled to myself and thought of the good doctor. She was right after all. We did need a break from the madness. I pictured her pretty face and bright smile in my mind and instantly felt guilty. My wife was struggling with demons and drug addiction and here I was daydreaming about the beautiful doctor. I felt like a piece of crap, but I couldn't shake the thoughts I kept having of Doctor Turley. What a dilemma. I dozed off in my hotel room with the image of the good doctor in my mind's eye.

Meanwhile back at the facility Doctor Turley was deep into her treatment plan. Melody was strapped to an upright bed with electrodes protruding from all over her head and body. She was in a sedated stupor incoherently mumbling. An adjacent room was equipped with a control panel of sorts and a huge two-way mirror for observing Melody or any "subject" unlucky enough to find themselves in that bed. Melody was subjected to shock treatments and experimental drug treatments. The good doctor was literally torturing my wife and I had no clue. These so-called treatments were breaking Melody down mentally, and physically. While in Colorado I had called to check on Mel, and Doctor Turley was ecstatic as she explained the progress that they were making with Mel's treatment. I remember feeling very encouraged after the phone call. I happily relayed the info to my kids. We continued our little vacation secure and happy in the thought that Mel was getting better. We camped in the mountains under the starry night sky. It was so beautiful and relaxing. Chris asked me if his mom would be back to normal like before his Grandma had passed? I didn't know how to answer that question but I told him that everything would be back to normal soon. What a lie that turned out to be.

It was refreshing to be in Denver surrounded by family, surrounded by love and happiness. Every day was a party of sorts. We hadn't been around our Colorado family in years, so every visit was turned into an event. The kids loved it and so did I. We were enjoying this respite despite what was going on in our personal lives back in Dayton. I was determined to let my kids have fun and just be kids on this trip. They had been through so much with watching their mom deteriorate into whatever she had become. I couldn't put a name to what she was right now, but we were all such sad cases before this little getaway. I had begun to question my own sanity lately with the blackouts, and crazy dreams filled with murder and violence. Hopefully when we return home things will start to get back to normal. Maybe Melody will get better and come home better than ever. Maybe my mind will clear and I won't have any more blackouts. Those were some pretty big maybes', but still I was optimistic.

About ten days later we returned to Dayton tired, but happy and anxious to see Melody. Her progress was astounding according to Doctor Turley. When we arrived at the facility, she met us and explained how things were going. "The voices have not been back" she stated "and no crazy or aggressive behavior". To say that I was shocked is an understatement. "I believe these kinds of episodes can damage any normal persons mental and emotional wellbeing Mr. Pierce" she continued. I think my mouth may have dropped open as I listened to the doctor. The doctor just looked at me and calmly stated "In any event I would like to test you and the children just to be sure". "Test us for what?" I asked somewhat testily. She was getting on my bad side now and I asked the kids to leave the room. "What the hell is" I began but she interrupted me. "Please Mr. Pierce calm yourself" she said smoothly with a smile. "I understand your apprehension but I'm on your side. We are on the same team" she stated. "I just want what's best for each of you guys sir" she continued. "Doctor Turley my children and I aren't the ones abusing drugs my wife Melody is" I stated firmly. She replied calmly "Sir drug addiction damages the entire family unit not just the abuser". I sat back and thought about what the doctor was saying. Maybe she was right I must admit at least to myself if not to anyone else that I had been blacking out and losing all recollection of the events that transpired.

"Ok Doctor Turley let's do this" I said with more enthusiasm than what I actually felt. "Hell, what do we have to lose?" I continued. Over the next few days, the children and I were put through a series of tests and questionnaires that sort of grinded everyone's gears to be completely honest. We were all hoping for the best, so we did whatever the doctor asked of us. After a couple of intense days of testing the doctor sat me down and flatly told me that I was schizophrenic. I just stared at her blankly at a loss of words because I never expected her to say anything like that. "What are you talking about doctor?" I stammered. "Now remain calm Mr. Pierce" she stated calmly. "Your mind state is normal for what you have been going through" she continued. "Your children are damaged mentally and emotionally as well, but I'm worried for you sir" she uttered succinctly. "I am fine Doctor Turley" I replied somewhat shakily. "I can certainly appreciate your concern but please remember why we are here in the first place" I continued more steadily. "My wife and children are all that matter to me. Please help them because I will be fine "I said almost yelling. Doctor Turley stared at me for several moments as if she was in deep contemplation. Finally, she spoke softly as if to an injured child "Mr. Pierce I apologize if I have offended you. I assure you that that was not my intention, but please understand that I have a duty as a doctor to relay upon you my expert opinion". I heard the good doctor and maybe I did need help but right now was not the time for us to be working on me and my mental health. I stood up and left her office without glancing back.

The kids wanted to go back over my sister's house after we were done with all of the testing. I needed to clear my head with some alone time so I agreed and dropped them off at my sister Yvonne's house. As I drove home, I thought about everything the doctor had told me. Her concern felt genuine and she was in fact a head doctor. Still I felt a tinge of guilt for garnering attention to myself during my family's crisis. I showered and relaxed with a couple shots of cognac before falling into a deep refreshing sleep. I awoke the next day in a positive mind state feeling like a million bucks. I thought about what Doctor Turley had said and I was determined to at least give everything she was considering an honest try. I gave the doctor a call and scheduled a time to meet with her. The doctor sounded excited to hear from me, and the thought crossed my mind that perhaps she was feeling me you know? But anyway, she told me to come in to see her at my own convenience, so I told her about 1pm would be good for me. She agreed and we hung up. After the phone conversation I thought about what it would be like to sex Doctor Turley. Was she a nasty freaky type, or was she the lay there lazy type? Or maybe she was somewhere in-between on the freak spectrum. Personally, I like em extra freaky and nasty. My obscene thoughts were rudely interrupted by a news story on the radio. The radio was low volume, but I heard the man say "The police are looking for multiple suspects in a city-wide drug war that has been raging for the past several weeks. 13 men are dead so far and more murders are expected in retaliation."

I can't explain why that news story caught my attention. I mean it is sad that people are being killed, but they're drug dealers and gang bangers. They signed up for that lifestyle, right? I really wanted to catch back up on those perverted thoughts that I was having, but it was not to be. My daughter Shannon called asking about her mom. I told her that I was going to check up on her mom that very afternoon. I asked her what her little brother Chris was into. "Running around pretending to be a ninja. He is so annoying" she complained dryly. I laughed happily feeling a small sense of normalcy. Normal had been missing from our lives for so long it seemed. It is funny how bad times seem to last so much longer than they actually do, and the bad times seems so much worse than they actually are. Normally anyway. That last part was in most cases because what we were going through really was horrible. Conversely the good times, the fun times always feel fleeting and short lived, but those good times are remembered as if they were the best times ever. I wanted to cling onto some of the good times we had before Melody fell off. I smiled to myself as I reminisced and remembered the love I felt for my wife. Whatever I have to do I will do to get my family back to the way it was before these demons arrived in our lives.

When I arrived at the doctor's office, I felt guilty thinking about what I wanted to do to the doctor. Looking at the beautiful woman's face made it even worse. "Mr. Pierce would you be willing to talk with me and tell me what's been happening with you? Not just your day to day but your mental and emotional feelings as well?" she asked me matter of factly. I agreed to comply with whatever she wanted to do. "You cannot hold anything back sir" she began earnestly. "The only way I can help you and your family is to know the real about what you are really going through Alan" she continued seriously. She had said my name. She called me Alan. All of the sexual thoughts and perverse feelings toward Doctor Turley returned in earnest, and I was truly struggling to focus and be professional. I felt like a schoolboy crushing on his teacher knowing that she was always out of reach. Was Doctor Turley out of reach? Did I have a shot? "Let's go check on your wife" she said with care. Once again, the guilty feelings waved over my conscious. And suddenly, the thought came to mind that maybe I was just lonely and extremely horny. That's why I keep having delusions and fantasies about Doctor Turley. That made me feel a lot better because it made perfect sense. It has been several weeks since I had even sniffed a poonani so naturally I am horny.

Melody looked very well. I mean it was quite shocking actually. She was almost the old Melody again. But something was missing from her personality, and I couldn't put my finger on it at that moment. Maybe it was part of her recovery. I was just glad to see her looking somewhat like her old self. "How are you baby?" I asked as I hugged her close to me. "I'm feeling a lot better honey, just very tired all the time right now" she replied sleepily. "The kids have been worried about you Mel. Don't you want to see them?" I asked her. "Not today Alan. Tomorrow would be better please" she replied. "Ok no worries. I will bring them to see you tomorrow" I stuttered. And just like that she went and laid back down and closed her eyes almost instantly sleeping. "Wow" I thought to myself. As the doctor and I walked toward her office I asked her about Melody's condition. "How long will she be tired like that doc?" I asked her with concern. "That depends on your wife Alan" she replied with certainty. "The medications she is taking cause drowsiness, but for how long and how much she takes of these medicines depend on her acceptance and adaptation to living drug free" she continued professionally.

"Now let's talk about you Alan" she said cheerfully. I was apprehensive to say the least. I mean let's face it, I truly believed that something was very wrong with me mentally. Maybe it was the stress of everything that was going on, I don't know. What I did know was that I wanted my family back and that x'd out any and all other priorities. "Ok doc let's do this" I responded apprehensively. "Don't worry Alan we are just trying to iron out any feelings of guilt that you may be having." she responded seriously. "I think that you are feeling like this whole situation is your fault, and that just isn't the case." she continued "You are a victim Alan. Please relax and let me help you." she said kindly. So I relaxed and began at the beginning to let her know how we came to meet. About how Mel's mom dying triggered this entire sequence of events. About our children, and about the blackouts. I told her about the drugs, the pills, about how I had enabled her. I told her about how life was before we lost her mom. I held nothing back and to be perfectly honest with you it felt so good to let it all out. It felt like a tremendous weight was lifted off my chest and I could breathe better than I had breathed in months.

Doctor Turley heard me out and she made notes on her notepad. After several moments she asked me about the blackouts. "Alan what can you remember from the blackouts?" she asked. "Doctor Turley it's very strange, but I can't remember anything from those episodes. It's like I fell asleep and woke up without any recollection of what occurred during that time." I told her. "A few times I dreamed that I was a ninja hunting down demons and chopping them up into small pieces" I concluded slowly. She jotted in her pad and finally asked me "Would you be ok with being hypnotized Alan?" "I really don't believe in all that hocus pocus Doc." I responded with a chuckle. "But I'm here to try and make our lives return to some sense of normalcy, so I will try just about anything to get my family back." I told her sincerely. "Good Alan I just want you to try and have an open mind." she responded seriously. "This treatment can be very beneficial if you let it" she continued. "I will do my best Doc" I responded.

The person that was going to hypnotize me was a woman, and she was strikingly beautiful as well. "Oh my goodness where the hell do they get all of these fine ass women?" I thought to myself. Doctor Turley introduced us. Her name was Tina. I offered her my hand and she shook it with a smile. Tina had me lay back on a lounge chair of sorts. It was different than any chair or couch I had ever seen, but very comfortable. She explained everything that we were about to do. Doctor Turley sat down unobtrusively on the opposite side of the room with her trusty notebook. I called myself listening very intently to this fine ass Tina lady, but I dozed off. She woke me up gently nudging me, and I noticed that she was wearing a very pleasant perfume. I blinked a few times to clear my vision and I was once again taken aback by her beauty. She looked concerned; however, and I asked her if everything was ok. My voice seemed to settle her because she gave me a half smile and a nod yes. I sat up feeling like a million bucks. I began to wonder how I could get both of these women in the bed at the same damn time, and I smiled inside with that pleasant thought.

Doctor Turley interrupted my daydream "Alan let's take a walk and talk" she said ominously. At least it felt ominous to me at the time, maybe I was tripping because my mind was stuck on the threesome. As we walked outside around the grounds, I noticed how lovely the day was. So sunny and beautiful, not a cloud in the sky. Doctor Turley seemed hesitant to speak. I let her take her time even though I wanted to hear what she had to say. Finally, she said "Alan while you were under you spoke of killing several men in great and gory detail". I stopped in my tracks after hearing her statement. "I was under?" I asked stupidly. "Yes, you were under for over 2 hours Alan. It was like opening up the flood gates of your mind and you kept going and going and going" she responded. "You scared the shit out of poor Tina" she continued with a chuckle. "She was visibly shaken by your testimony" she continued. I was frankly speechless. How do you respond to hearing something like that? "It was just a dream right doc?" I asked her. "Normally I would speculate that you were in fact dreaming or fantasizing about murdering the people you felt had done you wrong" she began seriously.

"But with all of the unsolved murders all over the news right now I am intrigued Alan" she continued. "Your outward personality is one of a quiet, reserved, rational man who avoids confrontation at all costs" she began earnestly. "But you have another persona Alan. One that is ruthlessly violent and maniacal" she continued.

While Doctor Turley told me about myself, I felt a chill down my spine as I remembered back to when I had awakened on the kitchen floor covered in mud and blood. In my heart I knew that what she said was true. "Why can't I remember any of it doc?" I asked her. "Your subconscious mind is protecting you from the dark side of your personality Alan" she replied. "I have never experienced anyone with your level of psychosis Alan, and I am both excited and thrilled but also saddened" she stated excitedly. "I am beholden to you and your family because I'm your doctor, but I'm also supposed to protect society from, psychopathic murderers like yourself" she continued still excited. As she was speaking, I was beginning to wonder about Doctor Turley. Here she is telling me about how much of a killer I was and at the same time she was thrilled. "The real fine and smart bitches are always the ones that are fucking nuts" I thought to myself. "So what shall we do Doctor Turley? Shall I turn myself in to the cops and confess to killing those men?" I asked her. "I don't really know what we should do at this point Alan. I just hope that you aren't inclined to hunt down and kill any more drug dealers at the moment" she stated calmly.

I had to sit down and think about everything that had transpired. "Why am I killing drug dealers Doc? Is it because of my wife's drug addiction?" I asked her seriously. She looked away in thought before replying. "Yes and no Alan. I believe that you think that if you kill all of the drug dealers that were involved with your wife that she will somehow be saved and cured. I'm only postulating here because I don't know if your wife ever dealt with the men you killed. I am inclined to believe that she did in fact deal with each one of these individuals at one time or another and that's why you killed them. Once that trigger was pulled a ruthless yet cunning killer was unleashed. She was talking about triggers and all of this bullshit while I am wondering about what was going to happen to my kids. My poor babies had two fucked up parents. A drug addicted mom and a murderer dad. I was incredibly sad at this point because I started to wonder about the men I had killed. What kind of life were they living before I snuffed it out? What about their families? What about their kids? This was just too fucking much to deal with. I needed to smoke a joint or a blunt or something to calm my mind. Doctor Turley must have been reading my mind because she offered me a drink back in her office.

"This is a lot to take in Alan. Please think long and hard about where you want to take this from here" she said calmly. "What do you mean doc? I have to turn myself in and confess to killing those men" I said irritably. "No, no you don't" she spoke very softly almost soothing. "Doctors can't share their patient's information" she continued. "Your secret is perfectly safe with me Alan" she spoke with such care that I began to calm down and really analyze this situation. "Can't I plead insanity or some shit?" I asked her. She sat back in her chair and sipped on the expensive cognac in her glass before responding "I want to help you Alan. I believe that with the proper treatment you will be fine" she continued. I swallowed my drink and thought about what the doctor was saying. "Are you saying that I should get away with murder doc?" I asked her seriously. She smiled at that comment before responding "Alan you are sick. You have a mental disability that will not be treated properly by just sending you to prison". She stopped talking to pour both of us another drink. I swallowed that one too and she poured me another before sitting back down.

"I'm willing to jeopardize my life and career to make you into the man you were before all of this madness began" she stated firmly. "Why Doctor Turley? Why would you do that for me?" I asked her sharply. "Because I'm a Doctor Alan, and that's what doctors do" she responded kindly. I was taken aback by her offer and her candor. "I have worked and waited my entire life for a situation like this Alan" she told me. "Now I have the chance to actually put my theories to a real-life manifestation, and very frankly I am excited to do it" she concluded. I listened to her and thought about everything that she was saying. I was hesitant because of the seriousness of this entire dilemma. This was real life not some fucking science project for Doctor Turley to be awarded for years later. My children, and my wife matter too much for me to be playing with their lives. So, I explained how I felt and what my fears were to the doctor. “Alan I really do understand where you are coming from, and I want you to trust me when I say that I am here to help you not hurt you” she told me. “What can I do to convince you that I mean every word that I say to you? “she asked me seriously. I thought about it, but my mind was scrambled like eggs at the moment, so I told her that I would sleep on it and make a decision the next day.

When I got home my mind wandered all over the place. I was truly scared as hell. I could spend the rest of my life in prison, or I could give the good doctor’s plan a try. Poor Mel, would she come out of this better or worse? Would my children grow to hate me for leaving them parentless? This entire situation was overwhelming. I felt like a ton of concrete was sitting on my chest, and I began to weep very hard punching my head at the same time for its covert deceit. The GHETTO BOYZ song came to mind because my mind was playing tricks on me. I finally passed out into a restless sleep tossing and turning and dreaming. I dreamt of brighter days and happier times. I listened as my children played and laughed, and it brought a smile to my face. When I woke up, I felt a profound sadness about my life. I was glad that my kids were staying with my sister, because they didn’t need to see me like this. I looked at my reflection in the mirror as I brushed my teeth and washed sleep from my face. I looked bad. I decided that I would try the doctor’s plan. Even if it afforded me just a little bit of time to set everything up for my family to be financially secure it would be worth it. That brought a slight smile to my face as I imagined living my life always knowing that I was a step away from finishing my life behind bars, so I decided to live each day like it was my last day of freedom.

I made myself some breakfast that consisted of coffee, bacon and eggs, and cheese grits. My mind at ease now that I had decided which way to go. The phone rang and interrupted my thoughts. It was Doctor Turley on the phone sounding uncharacteristically hysterical. “Alan you must leave your home right now and meet me at my office” she was almost screaming into my ear. “What’s wrong Doc?” I asked her loudly. “Don’t ask questions Alan. Just go get into your car right this instant and go to my office. I will meet you there” she said hurriedly. Then she hung up the phone. Well this was very surprising to say the least. The doctor was always so cool, calm, and collected. I turned off the stove and grabbed my keys and headed to my car to go meet her. When I began to back out of my driveway a police car skeeted to a stop blocking me in the driveway. The officers jumped out of the car with their guns aimed at me yelling "Get out of the car with your hands in the air!"

I was booked into the Montgomery county jail on suspicion of murder in the first degree. Everything was blurry to me at that time. Once again, the dreamlike aura took over my consciousness and it was like I was looking down on myself from above. What I didn't realize at the time was that the hypnotist Tina had ran to the cops as soon as she had left our session. One of the dealers that I had killed was her cousin, so she wanted justice. It was big breaking news too with the Chief of police giving a statement to reporters. I found all of this out later from some of the other inmates I was celled with. I was also made aware of the fact that Tina wasn't the only person out for justice. Those dealers I had killed had friends and family that wanted my head on a platter. How could you blame them? They were right to feel hate towards me. I had murdered those men and now their peers wanted to murder me. So what if I did not remember killing them, so what if I was mentally ill, the Bible calls for an eye for an eye. At this point I just wanted it all to go away, end it Lord I said in my mind. As if on cue I was attacked and stabbed several times while waiting to use the phone in the day room.

I was taken to the hospital and stitched up and treated for my wounds. Was I going to have to live my life with my head on a swivel? When I arrived back at the jail, I was placed in a cell alone and away from the other inmates. Protective custody was what they called it. Doing time was already going to be hard but doing all of my time alone was going to drive me crazier than I already seemed to be. I was not given a bond, so I was waiting to be arraigned and hopefully get a bond from the judge. Doctor Turley came to visit me. She looked so sad that I felt sorry for her even though I was the one going through it. "I'm so sorry Alan" she began. "I had no idea that Tina would do something like this" she continued. "Her career as a hypnotist in this state is over" she stated angrily. "What's up doc?" I said with my best BUGS BUNNY impersonation trying to lighten the mood. She stared at me for a moment before responding while shaking her head. "You are amazing Alan. Here you are in jail accused of several murders, and after getting attacked you can still be joking around". "Hey, it can't get any worse right?" I asked her redundantly. "May as well make the best of this and try to figure out my next move" I continued earnestly.

Detectives visited me shortly after Doctor Turley had left. They were cool enough I guess under the circumstances. They asked me about the murders and my motive for committing them. I played dumb of course, or maybe I was just dumb. At this point I was living right on the edge of consciousness, a dead zone if you will. I truly couldn't tell the difference from when I was awake or if I was asleep dreaming. I think the interrogation continued for several hours. I vaguely recall being punched and yelled at, but like I said it was difficult to discern whether I was dreaming or awake. Some of my injuries were reopened by the kind detectives and I had to be stitched back up. The doctors made sure that I was pain free after the ordeal. I realized at that point right before my mind succumbed to the pain medication that it was all real. I really had been getting interrogated and I really had just caught a serious beat down. Again. I drifted off into thoughts of me and my kids vacationing together. Enjoying life. Enjoying each other's company.

I woke up the next morning in severe pain. I couldn't tell if it was from the stabbings or the concrete I had to sleep on, or the beat down I had received courtesy of Dayton's finest. The meds I received at the ER had worn off and I did not have any pain medication, so I tried to ignore the aching by busying myself getting ready to see the judge. My attorney came to see me and go over what was in front of us presently. "I have asked for an immediate dismissal of all charges Mr. Pierce. Your doctor's negligence in allowing for your personal treatment and private discussions to be leaked publicly is inexcusable" he told me sternly. "Your life and the lives of your family are in danger because of it" he continued. He explained to me about how I could protect myself and my family from the backlash these various drug dealers wanted to make me feel. He also said I should consider filing a suit against Doctor Turley. At the hearing the judge did in fact drop all charges noting that there just wasn't sufficient evidence to pursue this case. What a person says while hypnotized cannot be held against him or her. All of this was music to my ears. I was released and Doctor Turley was there to pick me up.

The doctor was very talkative in the car. She told me about how Tina had been fired. She also still wanted to treat me for my obvious psychosis. I told her that my family and I were moving away immediately. "It's too dangerous for us to be here doc" I told her. "I have family in Colorado that we can visit with while we sort all of this out" I continued. She told me that she understood how I felt and that she would do whatever she could to help. As we approached my home, we could see several emergency vehicles packing my street. My house was burning out of control. I got out of the car and watched as all of my belongings went up in flames. I approached an officer and told him who I was and that that was my home before asking him what happened. "Looks like arson sir. I am sorry for your losses" he said. Damn! What else can happen? I thought to myself. "I'm so sorry Alan" said Doctor Turley. Yeah me too I thought. Me too. I stood there staring at the wreckage and debris long after the fire trucks were gone. Sadness was being replaced with a dull feeling of anger. Maybe we won't move I thought. Maybe I will send my wife and children away while I stay and deal with this war that I had inadvertently started.

At least my vehicle was untouched, and I said a prayer for that, thanking God for sparing my car. I needed to go check on my family especially my kids. Mel was probably safe at the hospital, but my kids were at my sister's house. I drove there directly needing to make sure that they were ok. As I approached her house an overwhelming sinking feeling deep inside my belly overwhelmed me. A familiar and terrifying picture of emergency vehicles once again. This time at my sister's house where my children were. I stopped my car and jumped out running towards the carnage that was once my sister's beautiful home. The house had been shot up. I mean it was bullet holes everywhere. I began to weep as I asked where my loved ones were to the nearest officer. He looked at me and I must have looked pitiful because he couldn't even look me in my face again. He told me that my sister was shot, both of my kids were shot, and that my sister's husband was deceased. He told me the hospital they were at and I raced over there. As I drove to the hospital all I could see was all of their faces in my mind.

"Please God let them be ok" I spoke aloud to the heavens. I was allowed to see Chris immediately because he was in stable condition. Shannon and my sister were both in surgery. Chris was sedated and sleeping peacefully. Tears flowed as I held his small hand in mine. I asked how long the surgery would take and the nurse wasn't sure. What have I done? That thought blurred through my mind, then was replaced with another thought. Or more than a thought, a feeling. A feeling of red-hot rage. I wanted to see what Shannon and Yvonne's status was, but I couldn't breathe. I needed some air in my lungs, so I walked outside to clear my head. I was not feeling well at all. All I could think about was my poor babies and my poor sister. I couldn't take back what has happened, and there was no going back to what was before. My life would never be the same. I stood outside the hospital for about 25 minutes thinking about the grim future. The nurse walked out to me to tell me that both Shannon and my sister had passed away on the operating table. I blacked out then. I can't remember anything from that point until I awoke at Doctor Turley's house in her driveway.

She was at my car door knocking on it in a panic. Her knocking is what woke me up. "Where have you been Alan?" she asked. "No one has seen or heard from you in four days" she continued. I looked at her then. "Four days?" I repeated incredulous. "Yes, and there's more. There were four more drug dealers killed over that span, and the cops are looking for you heavy. "she told me. She then pulled me from the car and took me inside of her home. "Can you remember anything Alan?" she asked me. I just shook my head no because my voice would not work at the moment. The doctor undressed me and gave me a hot bath like she was my mother. I was still speechless allowing her to do what she wanted. "Is that better?" she asked me sweetly. I just grabbed her and kissed her fiercely holding her tight in my arms. After a long moment I released her "Yes a lot better now thank you" I replied. For a moment I thought that she was going to slap the shit out of me, but she just stared at me strangely for a while before grabbing my face and kissing me passionately. The next several hours were spent making sweet love and cuddling and talking. We both were feeding off the other's energy and I needed her sweetness. And boy was she sweet. I kissed and licked her entire body spending extra time at her pussy. I lapped up her juices like a thirsty hound. Her reaction pushing me to suck on her clit until she screamed for me to stop. I could tell she was feeding off of my sorrow because tears were running down her face as we loved each other back to life. We both obviously needed this respite. Finally exhausted we both fell into a deep coma like sleep.

When I awoke Madeline was in the kitchen making breakfast, it smelled good and my stomach started to rumble from the aromas. "Good morning Madeline" I said cheerfully. She turned and smiled at me. "Good morning yourself Alan" she responded. "Please call me Maddy, no one calls me Madeline" she chuckled. As we talked and ate our food, she began to tell me about everything that she learned from my being hypnotized. Apparently, I had begun the murder spree after discovering Melody in our living room sucking some guys' dick. She postulated that this particular incident broke something in my psyche, and the absolute horror of what I was doing was too much for my conscious mind to endure; therefore, the demons were created, and amnesia set in. I listened intently thinking about it all, and it made sense. Still I couldn't remember any of it as hard as I tried. She told me that the only way to recollect those events was to tap into my sub-conscious mind through hypnotism. Well I wasn't going down that rabbit hole again I thought to myself. The next bitch might auction my ass off to the highest bidder.

"What about those other killings?" I asked her. "Did I mention anything else?" I continued. "Oh yes" she uttered. She described how a small group of dealers were chased from the first facility Melody was at, and how the doctor told me about it. Subsequently dismissing Mel from his rehab with the suggestion that I try Groves mental health facility. She told me how I had hunted down the men and ruthlessly murdered them. I asked her how I was doing all of that without being awake. "You were quite awake and aware Alan" she said cautiously. "You have an alter ego or split personality if you will" she continued. Then she explained how my other self was called ILL. Just one-word ILL. I found it incredibly ironic that my alter ego would be called ILL since that's exactly what I truly was. The explanation continued however, "your buddy ILL has a very elaborate network of homes, cars, and weaponry Alan" she told me. Apparently ILL has been planning all of this for some time and he did it without letting me know about it. He even gives you an alternate ideal to explain in a nonsensical manner all of these murderous events that you can't remember. So while ILL is in killer mode you are dreaming of demons. When the doctor at that other facility was telling you about the dealers you were made to believe that your wife was just talking in tongues or voices or whatever.

She told me that I had been suppressing deep seated resentment since the drug abuse began. My own mild manner was the creator of ILL. "Each of us has a natural instinct to protect ourselves not only physically but mentally and emotionally as well" she explained. "While you as Alan are calm, cool-headed, and gentle; ILL is the almost total opposite" she said gently. "So ILL is my protector Doc?" I asked. She shook her head without speaking just looking at me closely. Maybe she thought that I was gonna unleash ILL on her ass. I told her that I would never harm her, and she laughed at that. "I'm worried about you Alan, not me I know that you wouldn't hurt me" she blurted out. I wondered how she could be so sure, but I kept that thought to myself. This beautiful woman had bathed me, sexed the shit out of me, and fed me so I wasn't going to spoil the mood. I actually could go for another round if she was up to it. She must have been reading my mind because she gently grabbed my hand and led me to the bedroom. "You have to go talk to the police Alan, and they may keep you for a while so I will give you something to hold you over just in case you have to stay locked up for an extended period. Hopefully not too long though" she uttered playfully.

We sexed for some time and it was wonderful. It felt like our bodies had melded together as one, and I wasn't just deep inside of her, she was also inside of me. I was so hard inside of her womanhood it felt like I was the hardest I had ever been, and I could feel her pulsate on my shaft as I stroked slowly at first then harder and faster as we loved each other. She was just as excited as I was because her juices were flowing like a river of extasy. Flowing all over my manhood and onto the sheets leaving a stain like she had peed in the bed. The sounds coming from each of us was something more than primal. We moaned with pleasure, and her pussy was sounding like when my Granny stirred mac and cheese. This was without a doubt the best sex I ever had. Word to Kellz. I felt no guilt at all like I imagined I would. Clearly things were finished with Melody and I. Hell who am I kidding? Our relationship had been over for some time. Now with my sweet Shannon gone and my sweet sister Yvonne gone there was nothing to lose. I was ready to die, I even welcomed the thought of it. This kind and beautiful woman deserved better than a sick serial killer that's for sure. I wanted to let her know how I felt about it all, but she shushed me with her finger on my lips. "SHH we will talk after this is all over, but for now you needed this and so did I" she told me kindly. We washed the sex from our bodies, and she drove me to the station to talk with the detectives.

The detectives were not too keen on my recollection of the events leading up to this day. At first I thought that they were going to beat me up again. I told them that I was deeply saddened by the passing of my daughter and sister, so I had been drinking and drugging for the past several days. It was especially suspicious since four more men were killed during those days that I was missing. They explained that although it would be genuinely understood if I was in fact killing dope dealers, there was no room in Dayton for vigilante justice. We can't have a serial killer slash vigilante loose in our city Mr. Pierce they emphasized. They searched what was left of my home and my places of business and my vehicle looking for any clues. I guess ILL aint as crazy as I make him out to be, I thought to myself. That motherfucker was covering his tracks like a professional hit man. The cops were pretty cool under the circumstances, but I could tell they wanted to nail my ass. They offered me police protection since the drug dealers that were still alive wanted me dead. I just asked them to watch over my son and my wife. They released me and I caught a cab to Maddy's place. I was not going to get caught slipping again. Every son of a bitch that had something to do with the deaths of my loved ones was going to pay.

I had to find a way to link up with ILL I didn't need his protection anymore I needed us to be on the same page at the same time. Now I realize how crazy that must sound, with me wanting to communicate with myself about myself. But honestly how much of this story hasn't been crazy? I went into the bathroom and stared at my reflection looking for some clue as to how to bring ILL into the room with me. "Hey ILL I know you can hear me man. Can you and I kind of team up?" I spoke to my reflection in the mirror seriously. "We both need to be on the playing field at the same time my man" I continued stupidly. Nothing, not a peep, not a thought. What the fuck! I thought to myself. So I rationalized that since there was no immediate trigger as the good doctor would say, then ILL must lay dormant in my subconscious waiting for the moment he can awaken and commence to ass kicking or killing whatever the case may be. That bitch Tina started the retaliation which caused my sweet Shannon to lose her life, so maybe she can make ILL come out to play whenever I wanted him to. I needed to run this idea past Maddy first and see what she thought about it.

"Hell no!" Maddy shouted at me. "Are you fucking craz…." she stopped mid-sentence. "I hate that word" she continued after a brief pause. "But really Alan what makes you think that you can trust her after the last episode when she turned you in to the police?" she asked me seriously. She stopped talking and stared at me as I stared back at her in silence. "You're going to kill her, aren't you?" she asked me redundantly. "If she wouldn't have went to the cops and put this in the streets then my sister and daughter would still be alive, and Chris wouldn't be shot up in the hospital." I explained simply. "The bitch gots ta die" I said looking in her eyes for a clue as to how she felt about this. The other killings were made by ILL, but here I was openly discussing murder with Maddy the Doctor. Was she going to ride or die? I asked myself with a grim chuckle. This lady was no fool and each moment made me admire her more. "So what if I don't agree Alan?" she asked me her voice rising. "Are you going to kill me too? Tie up all your loose ends Alan?" she was screaming at me now. I wrapped my arms around her and kissed her forehead. "No baby I would kill myself before I ever hurt you" I whispered in her ear. One thing was clear to me all of a sudden. ILL and I had linked up. I couldn't say the exact moment, but I knew that he was with me. I could feel it and I had recollections that I hadn't had just hours ago. I thought to myself "It's on now motherfuckers!".

We hugged and kissed and talked for hours after the initial conversation about murder had passed between us. I think we were both reassured, or perhaps assured, I'm not sure, but it was like a veil had been lifted and we were now one. We were a team. And she wanted to win just as badly as I did. Why couldn't I have met this wonderful woman years ago I wondered to myself. Maybe this was God's plan for my life, maybe I had to go through everything that I had been through to get to this moment. Maybe that is the only way that I could or would truly appreciate the blessings and the pain. In my mind I visualized Shannon's smile, and the tears began to flow again. "Why my baby girl have to die Maddy?" I whimpered as my body shook with grief. "I wish it would have been me instead" I cried hard. Maddy held my hands and looked me in the eye. She told me what she thought we should do step by step like she had planned all of this beforehand. I didn't care. I listened and contemplated and finally I agreed with her plan. "Are you sure this is something that you want to do Maddy?" I asked her. "I want to make them pay for hurting you baby" she said seriously. That's all I needed to hear. Let's find Tina.

Tina was no fool she was nowhere to be found. I speculated that she had left the city, because it's not hard to find someone in Dayton. Maddy made some calls and confirmed that the bitch had in fact left town when she heard that I was free. Damn! This was inconvenient. I not only wanted to kill the bitch Tina, but I also needed information about the cats that were after me. I especially wanted to know who was responsible for killing my blood. I didn't know what she knew or whom she had told about our session, but I had to find out. As the day passed, Maddy's people came through and we finally received her location. She was staying with a family member in Muncie, Indiana. We Googled the spot and decided to hit the highway. It was only a couple of hours away, so I decided to check on Chris before we rode out. He was doing better thank goodness. Looking at my boy laying there in pain having come close to death himself made the rage return in earnest. It's time to get this party started I thought to myself. I was anxious to hear what info this bitch could give us. Maddy was quiet as we rode, and I wondered if she was having second thoughts now that this shit was about to go down. I turned on some music and concentrated on the task at hand. Kidnapping Tina wasn't part of the plan at first, but since this goofy bitch thought that she was going to get away with the deaths of my family it was part of the plan now. I reasoned with myself that if she did give me good info that I would make her death quick and painless. If on the other hand this bitch tries to play hard then I will stretch her death out for weeks. Torture her ass until she begs for death.

After we located the house, we drove by it before settling into a parking spot to watch for any movement. Maddy was alert now, and she was acting excited. The thought flashed across my mind that perhaps Maddy is a fucking basket case, but the thought dissipated almost immediately. How could I be calling someone a basket case when I really am a basket case. Maybe that was our bond. We would be Bonnie and Clyde crazy together forever. It wasn't long before we saw Tina come out of the house with another female that we guessed was her family member. They got into a car and drove off. Maddy got out of the car and walked to the front door of the house they had just left. She knocked on the door loudly. After a moment she knocked again. No one answered the door, so we surmised that no one was home. It was after 9pm and dark so we broke into the side door. We searched the house and it was in fact empty and thank goodness they didn't have a freaking dog. We searched for any weapons, and we found good hiding spots. For some reason or another we both became horny and proceeded to make love Gorilla style. That session calmed our nerves and we posted up to wait for their return. Maddy was very impressive. She knew what to do without being told. It was like we were connected mentally and spiritually. My love for her deepened as the moments passed by.

Several hours later we could hear them coming towards the house talking and laughing. It sounded like they had been out drinking because Tina's speech was slurred. My senses were heightened as I waited to pounce on these unsuspecting bitches. They entered the house still exuberant and silly. They had definitely been drinking because they came in laughing and talking and then suddenly after a short time it was silent. I waited a few minutes listening for movement. They had passed out drunk because I heard snoring. I peeked in at them to confirm what I was hearing. This was going to be easier than I thought, and I chuckled at our good fortune. We tied them up and gagged them and Maddy gave them something to help them sleep even better. I went and got the van while Maddy watched them snore. After we loaded them in the vehicle, I asked Maddy where we should take them. "I have a place in Yellow Springs out in the country" she said cheerfully. She loaded the address in my GPS, and we proceeded there chatting like high school sweethearts.

As we rode, I thought about everything that had happened to bring us to this point. I wanted to kill this Tina bitch so bad that I could taste it. I wanted to torture her, I wanted to shove foreign objects into her holes, I wanted to apply red hot metal to tender parts of her skin. The deaths of my daughter and sister outweighed any compunction of morality. My heart and my mind were cold like the metal benches I had to sleep on at the county jail. The only warmness remaining was for my sweet son and this sweet partner in crime I have now. I looked over at her and admired not only her beauty, but also her resolve to do exactly what she says she will do. Most people say shit that they really don't mean. They try to figure out what they think you want to hear and then try to spoon feed it to you like nasty medicine. Castor oil comes to mind because that shit is nasty and makes me gag like the so many lies I have been told by so many liars. The liar I was thinking of at the moment was Melody my wife. It stands to reason that if she had not become a fucking drug addict then ILL wouldn't have started killing people. All of the episodes of betrayal began to replay in my mind. All of the cheating on me in the name of drug addiction. Like that was supposed to make it better. Like I should overlook her transgressions because of her sickness. I made up my mind to kill that bitch also before this shit was over with.

Maddy's spot was perfect for what we were doing. I couldn't contain my surprise "Wow Maddy are you into farming?" I asked her smiling like a fat kid with cake. I mean this place was amazing. There were no neighbors within eyesight. It was surrounded by trees and wilderness. Just amazing. Now as amazed as I was with the place being remote, I was not prepared for what she showed me next. There was a shelter. An underground shelter originally built to escape tornadoes, and she had the space revamped and aesthetic. It was set up like a miniature operating room of some sort. I just looked around with my mouth agape looking quite stupid. She just smiled at me proudly then asked me what I thought about the place. I hugged her tightly and kissed her. "Baby we are meant to be together. I wish I would have met you years ago" I told her sincerely looking into her eyes before tongue kissing her passionately. All of a sudden, I wanted to have her right then right there. There were cots around the room I pushed her onto one taking her clothes off violently at the same time she ripped at my belt and pants until they were around my ankles. We made crazy noises as the emotions took over and sweat beaded on my forehead dripping into my eyes. We came together and I slumped down on her gloriously spent.

There was no denying that I had fallen hard for Maddy. She was literally the woman of my dreams. What more could I ever ask for? After we had strapped both women to cots we went up to the main house and relaxed, ate some food, then made love some more before falling into a deep restful sleep. I dreamed while I slept. I dreamt of better days with my family, and Shannon was so happy laughing and playing with her mom and brother. I stood back observing my happy family. "Alan you know that you need to be asking God for forgiveness" a familiar voice spoke behind me. I turned around to see my beautiful granny right there in the flesh. I bent down to hug her tightly as a tear ran from my eye. "You done let them demons get you boy" she cried at me seriously. "Now you done become a demon Alan" she said sadly. "I'm so disappointed in you boy, but you can still ask him for forgiveness. You can still repent Alan" she continued. I just held her in my arms crying hard knowing that the path that I was on was one of no return. Knowing that there was no going back now. My sweet Shannon had to be avenged. Revenge is mine sayeth the Lord, but this revenge had to be all mine I told myself. I woke up refreshed, but with a profound melancholy upon my mood. My granny was right of course. I had become a demon, but I had to finish this now. It was way too late to turn back now. It was at that moment that I remembered my grandmother's words and I knew without a doubt that having them demons on you was in fact the worst thing that could ever happen to a person.

I fiddled in the kitchen making coffee and scrambled eggs with toast because Maddy was still sleeping. The aromas must have wakened her because she came into the kitchen momentarily. "Wow you're up already?" she asked me cheerfully. "Yeah sleepy head" I replied grabbing her and kissing her. She pulled away laughing "No, no, no you animal. We have work to do today. Those bitches are awake by now and alert. It's time to get some answers" she told me. I agreed so we had breakfast, small talked before heading to the shelter. She was right, both of them were wide awake. Tina's eyes widened when she saw me. I walked over to her almost touching my nose to hers. I smiled at her discomfort "Hey Tina" I said loudly. "You owe me Tina. You owe me some answers" I continued. I explained to her that if she let me know whom she had talked to about me that her family member could be spared. I pointed to her mockingly "What has she done to deserve this?" I asked her redundantly. Tears flowed from Tina's eyes uncontrollably. I removed her gag so she could speak. "Please just let her go and I will tell you anything you want to know" she pleaded. I put the gag back in her mouth and pulled Maddy outside for a quick chat.

Once we were outside, I asked Maddy about truth serum. She laughed and told me that there really wasn't such a thing. She explained to me how people thought that sodium thiopental was some sort of truth serum, but that she had in fact tested the theory and found that while most people will be less evasive and more honest, that they are also more prone to suggestion. You can't be for sure if someone is telling you the truth or telling you what you want to hear she surmised. "Don't worry love I can bring out the truth from anyone" she told me confidently. I was starting to feel like this wasn't my party at all and that Maddy had manipulated this entire ordeal. But how could she have though? She could not have predicted meeting me and my family. She could not have anticipated in her wildest dreams that she would meet a psychopath such as myself, right? All of these thoughts and questions were running through my mind as I looked at her trying to see beneath the surface. The dream about my granny flashed across my mind like a distant thunder bolt flashing across the sky. I asked God to forgive me and reasoned with him that I would totally repent when this was all over with.

Maddy told me that she would take over from here and that she just wanted me to support whatever she was doing. That was fine by me because I just wanted results. She pulled up a chair next to Tina smiling at her as she did so. "Tina you played me. I really backed you up when every other doctor in this area scoffed at you" she began. "I wanted you to be a part of something great, but you fucked up Tina. And now here we are" she continued. "You should be grateful to Alan because I wanted to have you and your peoples included in my lab work. Well if you cooperate then Alan will take care of your family and let her go" she stated coldly. Tina knew that she was dead. There was no reprieve for her. She could perhaps save her family member though. I still didn't even know who this bitch was to Tina. "Maddy who is this bitch anyway?" I asked. Maddy looked back at me then turned slowly back to face Tina.

"Who is this bitch Tina?" she asked her chillingly. Both bitches were still gagged so neither could answer but the looks on their faces was priceless, and I was glad that Maddy had taken over.

Maddy was really good at this and I surmised that her background in mental cases was a tremendous help. She knew how to manipulate the situation psychologically, and it was working like a charm. She removed the gag from ol girl with Tina and asked her who she was. "I'm Shania" she stuttered. "Tina is my cousin. Her mom and my dad are siblings" she was stuttering like a mother fucker and it would have been laughable if not for the situation we were in. Maddy put her gag back in place silencing Shania. Then she got all up in Tina's face whispering "Bitch you tried to have my man killed. What happens to you is already sealed, but if you want your cousin Shania to live you better come correct". The look in Tina's eyes told a story, they told us that she was willing to do whatever we asked of her to save her cousin. Maddy took off her gag and let Tina speak for herself "Ok yall I will cooperate just please let Shania go first". She was pleading for her cousin even though neither of their lives was worth spit. I truly felt sorry for poor Shania, but that bitch had to die too. Wrong place wrong time for her. And it was sad for her, but I was not the slightest bit concerned about that bitch. I was a demon now. It was confirmed. I untied Shania's straps leaving her hands tied, stood her up and led her into another room. Then I drugged her and tied her back up. She was a cutie for sure. Such a waste I thought to myself before going up to the house for a bit.

I returned while Maddy continued with the interrogation, I looked on making mental notes. Tina spoke of a few names that could perhaps be upset with me about this turn of events, but I had already killed most of them only two of the guys still existed. One of them was a small fry named Mo. He called himself Goldie after the pimp. The other was a low-key baller named Starling. Starling had the resources to get at me, and I concluded that it was him all along. I went over in my mind the thugs that I had killed and the majority of them traced back to Starling. I thought about it all and it was totally logical that this nigga was pissed at me. To be perfectly honest I couldn't blame him for wanting me dead. I had interfered with his business. The men I had killed were dealing for him. My nigga ILL was very thorough. He had single handedly almost depleted the entire Dayton heroin drug dealers. The fact that I no longer needed him to conduct murderous adventures occurred to me. I looked at it as a passing phase that I had to go through. Now after I kill these two dudes I would retire from murder and killing and settle down with my baby Maddy. We could move away from Dayton. Hell, we could leave Ohio all together. Me, her, and Chris would start a new life in a new place.

Tina was telling us everything that we wanted to know. I felt as though this was as good a time as any to off the bitch. I wanted her to die for causing the death of my sweet daughter. Maddy had other plans because she pulled me outside with urgency. “What’s up baby?” I asked her a bit annoyed. “We can’t kill these girls just yet baby” she told me. Then she explained that she had treatments and drugs that were experimental and outlawed but would be perfect for our situation. After all aren’t these bitches as good as dead anyway? She reasoned with me. I really wanted the pleasure of killing that bitch Tina, but my baby said her life could be used for the greater good of mankind. I understood where my baby was coming from. She was a doctor with aspirations of being great. I was just a broken man turned demon that wanted revenge for actions probably attributed to me in no small fashion. I enabled Melody in the beginning. I was the one ignoring the signs while my babies tried to alert me to our predicament. Maybe it was the guilt that I felt that pushed me to keep going forward on this ominous path. I had to try and come to grips that I was to blame for my family’s plight. I was trying my best to project it unto those others that had fallen into this spider’s web of murder and infamy.

I walked outside to get away from the temptation. ILL was retired but he was no longer needed. I was very content to dish out this violence. Numbing my own guilt, numbing my pain was all that I wanted at this point and I thought that killing these people would bring me solace. There was no rational aspect to my thought process at this point. I was a full-blown demon in my own right now. Oh how disappointed my Granny must feel looking down from heaven on me. The thought occurred to me that my darling Shannon and Yvonne were there with my sweet granny, and that they were all looking down upon me in shame and disgust at my actions and attitude. The questions arose in my mind about Maddy. She had this place crafted and built just for something like this to occur. How long had she been planning, waiting on some unlucky test subjects? I wondered what her tests consisted of. Were they painful? What would she have done if I never came along with my crazy situation? My mind was overflowing with these thoughts as I struggled to remain focused on the path ahead of me. At least two more people were going to be murdered as far as I was concerned. Any extra killings would be attributed to the objects of my disconcert. As long as they were alone when the time came then I would not go out of my way to kill others. Sometimes a person's number comes up unexpectedly like Tina's poor cousin.

After some time had passed Maddy came outside to join me. She asked me if something was wrong or if I was bothered by anything. I asked her about all of the questions and concerns that I was experiencing. She explained to me that she had patterned her plan sort of like a horror movie. She had planned to get homeless vagrants at first to do her experiments on. She reasoned that they wouldn't be missed or raise suspicion. "Like I told you before love, I have dreamed but never could I have imagined you coming into my life. It's all my dreams coming true right before my eyes" she told me sincerely. She kissed me and whispered her gratitude. I explained to her that I was in mourning for my sister and especially my daughter Shannon. I tried to explain to her how the guilt that I felt was eating me alive. "That's why I want to kill someone right now" I explained. It made me numb for that brief moment of violence. That's the reason why ILL has not shown up anymore I reasoned. He could no longer protect me from the pain, or the tremendous blame I put on myself for all of this. I guess I still owe ILL a bit of gratitude despite the backlash. If not for him I would have still been getting spit on by Melody. Not in a literal sense of spit on, but in a figurative sense. Every time she cheated on me; she was spitting in my face. Every time she stole from me or lied to me; she was spitting in my face. The really wild thing about all of it was that I could not see it before. Was I stupid? Was I naïve? I was ranting I guess but Maddy listened to all of my pent-up emotions and hugged me when I cried. She never judged me or looked down on me for allowing Mel to destroy our lives. These days I cried a lot. Every time I thought of my babies being shot because of me; I broke down.

I could tell that Maddy did not like me suffering because she would always try to take my mind somewhere else away from my guilt and pain. "Let's go look for these niggas she mentioned baby" she said cheerfully. I asked her what she intended to do with the two girls tied up in the emergency cellar. "I have them both on IV drips administering drugs and fluids so they will be fine" she quipped. Tina thinks that you released her cousin so we will keep them in separate rooms until they are no longer necessary. Then we will give them a reunion before we kill them baby. That was fine by me because I had a feeling that one or both of these niggas had something to do with the retaliation towards my family and me. Especially that Starling nigga, I was convinced that he was responsible but I had to be sure. Murder was once again my focus. I knew where all of ILL's stash spots were now, whereas before I couldn't recollect any of it. Dude had us ready for war. He had established three different houses where he stashed guns and lump sums of cash. The money coming from the dead dealers. Hell, they didn't need it. If not for the bitch Tina everyone would have thought that this was a drug war or some shit so ILL always took all of the drugs and money from the dead dealers. Regardless I was grateful for all of this because it made my mission so much simpler. A scary thought flashed through my mind at that moment. "Maddy baby I want you to stay home. I could not live if something were to happen to you" I pleaded with her. She grabbed my hands with hers and looked into my eyes. "Baby I belong at your side for better or for worse, life or death. How do you think I would feel if you were killed?" she asked me. "From now until the day I die I will be right here with you through anything and everything" she stated seriously. How do you argue with that? Fuck it lets ride baby.

We rode up on the Mo guy without really even trying. I parked up the block while Maddy made the approach. She was going to drug the fool and volunteer him for more of her experiments. She promised that we would interrogate him and if he were in any way responsible for the shootings of my loved ones then I could burn him alive. I watched her work and I have to admit that she would have gotten my ass too. She was so smooth, so beautiful. I wager that even a gay man who did not like women would fall for her charms. And she was all mine. Wow is what I said to myself as the nigga started falling all over himself thinking he had bagged a real live one. I hopped into the back of the van and waited as they approached. I heard the conversation and I almost laughed out loud. This fool was downright giddy with enthusiasm. He opened the van door without even looking at me with my 45 pointed at his face. He noticed me too late "Just hop on in here lover boy" I laughed at him. Maddy hit him with the needle right below his ear into his neck. He slumped before getting settled into his seat. I just let him lay where he slumped.

After depositing Mo into the lab as we were starting to call the cellar, we made love and went to see Chris again before going out to eat. Like I said before our love making was out of this world. It is difficult to put the intense pleasure into words. I will say this and then I'm done trying to explain this woman's love. If I could bestow anything to every person on the planet, I would choose that every person be allowed to feel the ecstasy that I feel when I am inside of my baby. That feeling is beyond priceless. Fuck diamonds and gold and money. If I could just make love to Maddy every day for the rest of my days, then my life has been one for the ages. I wondered if she felt the same way. Coming inside my baby takes all of my troubles and grief away for an indeterminate amount of time. She was my pusher and my drug of choice at the same time. If this was wrong, then I did not want to be right ever again. I was in love yall and it was the best feeling next to the birth of my babies. I wanted to spend the rest of my life living for this woman, or at a moment's notice die for this woman. Bonnie and Clyde aint have shit on us. That's on God.

The next day we planned our routine. We knew what areas this Starling guy hung out in, so Maddy put on her work out gear and proceeded to go jogging through those hoods in hopes of catching his attention. Once again, my baby has proven herself to be a bad ass bitch because this nigga approached her on the drive by tip hollering out of his car window. "Excuse me miss may I run with you?" he yelled from his car. Maddy kept jogging ignoring him. Then he parked his car and started jogging beside her smiling stupidly at her. They continued up the block before stopping and talking. As I watched from afar, I wondered what he was saying to her. His hand and body gestures gave me the impression that he was trying really hard to bag Maddy. No one could blame him because Maddy was a fox and those leggings she had on should be against the law. They were both laughing as they started to walk towards his car. I smiled to myself like she done bagged another one. I started to picture in my mind exactly what I wanted to do to this motherfucker. I'm almost positive that Maddy has plans of her own. A garbage truck coming past blocked my view for a few moments. After it was gone, I looked and his car and my Maddy was gone too.

My first instinct was to panic and drive around to find them but I chilled myself out with a self-talk. I reasoned that Maddy could handle herself and she was probably improvising at the moment. I sat there for about 45 more minutes before driving to her place to wait for a signal of some kind. I can't even lie to yall I was genuinely worried about my baby. I rolled up a blunt to calm my nerves because at this point, I was stressing the fuck out. It had been over 2 hours and no word from my baby. What if something happens to my Maddy? What would I do then? I began to contemplate a future without Maddy and I just couldn't do it. She had grown on me and I needed her in my life. I began to pray for her safe return to me. Another hour or so passed before I heard a car approaching. I grabbed my 45 and ducked out of sight to observe the car's approach. It was moving kind of fast so I took my gun off safety. Whoever was driving being not a very good one I thought to myself. They slammed on the brakes and out jumps my baby yelling "ALAN! ALAN!". I ran from behind the bush towards her feeling my heart pound in relief. We embraced and kissed happily. I think I may have shed a tear of joy since Maddy was ok. "Come help me take him to the lab baby" she said.

After he was tied and gagged, we went up to the main house to talk. She explained to me what had happened, apparently, he was aware of how Mo had been captured and had devised his own plan to get us before we could get him. "I thought my goose was cooked baby" she yelled excitedly. She told me how he had pulled a gun on her and forced her to drive his car to an empty trap house. He was telling her that he wanted her to call me over there to get her. His plan probably would have worked on any other person but not my Maddy. He had under estimated her and she had given him a shot in the neck before he knew what happened. "I was waiting on my chance baby. All I could think about was getting back to you" she told me sincerely. "He turned his back and I had that needle in his neck instantly" she continued. So this motherfucker tried to get me again. He was going to pay for this shit. Maddy was reading my mind again because she explained that she had something special planned for him. "I have something planned for them all baby. Will you be my lab assistant baby?" she asked me coyly. I grabbed her close to me and kissed her and let her know that I would do anything she wanted me to do.

Maddy was a mad scientist in the true sense of the word, so when I left her to go and check on Chris, she smiled at me and told me she would see me soon and that she loved me. Chris was up and cheerful when I arrived. His smile made me happy and at the same time a sick feeling deep in the pit of my belly formed and made breathing difficult. I stepped into the bathroom so my son wouldn't see me crying. I was still sick with grief and no amount of murder would make it better. I rejoined Chris momentarily and we chatted and laughed together. As I watched my boy talk and laugh, I could tell that he was trying to cope with his loss also. Him and his sister were very close and he was his aunties favorite by far, so he was dealing with the pain as best as he could under the circumstances. He would be released the next day so we planned out what our next moves would be. I explained to him about Maddy and I, and surprisingly he smiled and laughed. "That doctor lady is pretty dad. I could tell that you liked her" he stated to his shocked father. The odd thing about our visit together was that he did not mention his mom not one single time. I figured that he would ask how she was doing or something but no he never said a word concerning his mother. I hugged him and told him how proud I was of him and his strength through all of this before leaving.

Two detectives were waiting for me as I was leaving the hospital. They were polite and a bit chatty. They spoke of the killings stopping over the last few days, and asked how I was doing. I wasn't really in the mood for chatter but I wanted to return the polite yet fake banter. I let them know that I was still in mourning and sad about my boy. After a few minutes of small talk, I tried to excuse myself from them but one of them asked me if I knew anything about the disappearance of Maurice Hicks aka Mo aka Goldie. Never heard of him was my response. How about Starling Mitchell? Or Tina Baxter and her cousin Shania? I just held up my hands and turned around to the wall to put my hands on it like I was being arrested. We aren't arresting you yet you sick son of a bitch but just know that we are watching you. Have a nice day. I stayed in that pose for a few seconds as they walked away. Sick son of a bitch?? Why would he say such things I thought to myself? But then the thought crossed my mind that I really was in fact very fucking sick. The shit I was doing is not normal. The shit Maddy and I are doing is not normal. How does one change after becoming a demon? Once that level of vile evil touches you it's just like losing your virginity. There is no going back for me. I looked to the heavens and said a silent apology to my loved ones there.

I took my time going back to Maddy's place even changing up cars in case they hit me with a GPS tracker. I wasn't followed but I was nervous non the less. Maddy was very busy with our guests, they were being poked, prodded, drugged, and shocked. She was obviously enjoying herself but all of this did nothing at all for me. I wanted to make one of these motherfuckers' bleed. Maddy informed me on the information she had gleaned so far. Mo and Shania were the innocent ones out of all of this, neither knew about me or my family. Tina had informed Starling about our session and he was responsible for killing my blood and leaving my boy shot up. I walked over to him watching his eyes as I approached. He had the look of a man who was accepting of his fate, he just wanted this to end. I went to pull my 45 and Maddy grabbed my wrist. "Please baby not yet" she pleaded. "After I'm done with him, he will beg you to blow his head off trust me" she said with relish. We went to the house to talk and eat and I told her about my visit with detectives.

Maddy reasoned that the police would probably be bugging me for some time after all that has happened. She smiled at me and began to tell me everything that she had planned for our guests. Those poor souls were better off with me putting a bullet in their brains. I let her know how I was feeling about all of it and how I just wanted to bleed Starling real slow. I let her know that I was picking Chris up from the hospital the next day, and being as our home was ashes, I wanted us to all stay together at her house in Dayton. She was fine with it, so we prepared a room for Chris at her home in the city. We began to make plans for the future. We would complete her sessions with our guests, then we would dispose of the bodies, then we would move away from Ohio. Start a new chapter in our lives together. I could easily go back to my regular life as a contractor. Chris would get well and grow up happy and healthy. I changed my mind about killing Melody, she had been through enough I reasoned after Maddy told me about the treatments she had subjected Mel to. We were divorced amicably.

We brought Chris home to what seemed like a normal household, a normal family unit you might say. Maddy and I continued the experiments and torture of our guests for several months. Of course, we kept Chris on a normal path. He went back to school, and he was once again super active like before. I spent as much time as I possibly could with him. My revenge was not complete however so I still attended to our guests sometimes just not as much as Maddy did. I waited patiently for the day that she would tell me that I could kill Tina and Starling. The day came unexpectedly to me but I could tell that Maddy had it all planned out. She was giddy as she told me about the completion of her tests and experiments. My appetite for violence had subsided somewhat after Chris had come home, but I could feel the thirst returning as she told me about how our guests time had run out. Mo and Shania were victims of circumstance I reasoned. Bullets to the temple was the mercy I showed them both. For Tina I reserved a special treatment. I abused her orifices with objects not meant for bodily use. Parts of her tongue were removed so her attempts at speech sounded like gibber jabber. After a time, she no longer even responded to her torture. We dropped her off on the east side of Dayton naked.

My main man Starling had his own special treatment session reserved just for him. Maddy had come up with a special course of drug cocktails for him and Tina. "After these drugs take effect, they won't be the same people at all" Maddy explained. "They won't even be able to remember their own names baby" she continued. So the plan was to torture them both and release them to a society with no patience for mental patients. The ultimate torture being for them both to live while not really living at all. They were both neutered and spayed like pets. There was going to be no continuation of either one of their respective species. Many people will think that I am being too cruel, but my losses are immeasurable therefor there is no limit to what these creatures shall endure. Fuck you sue me. After all of the torture and drug treatments I still felt empty. There was no filling the emptiness consuming my soul and being. Even when I drove through Dayton and watched as Tina and Starling were ostracized on the streets, homeless and destitute. One day while I was getting gas Tina was flagging cars down and flashing her tits as the cars drove by. I overheard a young lady speaking about Tina. "Girl she used to be so pretty and smart until somebody slipped her a mickey. Just so sad" she said. But I felt little if any satisfaction for their plight. My losses could never be repaid. My pain never salved. Now I truly understood why revenge is the Lords. I pray for forgiveness and I repent my sins.

Six years later Maddy and I are married and we have us a four-year-old daughter whom Maddy insisted that we name Shay out of love for Shannon. Chris is a senior in high school and he is doing absolutely terrific. I just couldn't be prouder of my boy. Shay was already a little prodigy taking after her mom as far as intelligence. Maddy was renown as a psychologist now her name was even being mentioned in talks for the Nobel prize. Her treatments were now famous worldwide for their effectiveness. The saying being that "If Doctor Turley couldn't fix you then you just can't be fixed". I was extremely proud of my baby. We had both come so far. I was no longer a contractor I taught classes about becoming a contractor. Maddy had accumulated so much wealth over these last few years that I only taught to keep myself busy and to share my knowledge. Maddy has cured me of my guilt and pain to a degree that is bearable. I spend each day praying and thanking God for bringing us through the ordeal we had suffered. We attend church service each and every Sunday now.

Every so often I will think back on how we came to be where we are today, and I will think about the demons, and I will think about ILL. I will think about my sweet sister and my darling Shannon and I may even shed a tear. Maddy told me that the pain will remain with me until I die, but that I can't let it control my life. She taught me coping skills. My Granny never left me though and I stopped being a demon. I still dream of my Granny sometimes and she still loves me. She is proud of me for getting the demons up off of me. And she still warns me to stay strong in Christ because the demons can and will come back if you let down your guard. So here we are today living in Colorado. I wanted us to be close to family. We have moved on from the craziness of demons and drugs. Thank God and thank my sweet beautiful grandmother.

Meanwhile in Dayton, Ohio a vagrant guy has been arrested for exposing himself to a group of children. In the county lock-up he receives a beatdown for being weird and for messing with kids. He awakens in the hospital mumbling incoherently about being kidnapped and tortured by Alan and his bitch doctor girlfriend.

Entanglement

I wake up pissed off. For one thing I hardly slept at all, and for two this mother fucker has stayed out all night. AGAIN!! He had the audacity to turn off his phone because I was blowing that thing up. It's the first week of August and the summer is almost over. Cuffing season is on the way. Why can't he be a man about it and just tell me what he wants to do? This shit has gotten old, and I get tired of hearing the same excuses. If his punk ass didn't pay all my bills, I would have been left his sorry, cheating ass a long time ago. I'm going to get me a job and start saving my money. Life is too short for this type of bullshit. I'm young, attractive, and we don't have any kids together so there really is nothing holding me back. We just have history if that's what you want to call it. We have been fucking around for six years give or take a few months here and there, and it's had it's good and bad points, but lately he has been taking me for granted. I can tell he cheating because we don't fuck like we normally do. He's always gone talking about he getting money. He must really like whatever little bitch he fucking with this time because he has stayed out all night like three times in the past couple weeks. Let me pack up my shit, fuck it I will stay with my mom for a while until I get my shit together.

My name is Kierra but everyone calls me Key. I just turned 22 years old July 21. My sorry ass soon to be ex-boyfriend has been in my life since I was 15, but we never messed around until I turned 16. He's older than me by a few years, he's 32. Yeah, I know he was 25 when we first met, but I just never liked guys my age. When I was 15 it was easy for me to tell people that I was 18 or 19. My body was developed at that time already, so older guys were always flirting with me and trying to get on. Justin is the sack of shits name. I'm getting me a job and getting me a new man too. Fuck Justin with his no-good two-timing ass. Let's see how he likes it when I cut his ass off for good. My girlfriend Kenia and I were going around town putting in job applications. We were pretty close I have known Kenia almost my whole life. Since we were about 6 or 7 years old. "Girl I told you that Justin wasn't shit" she was laying it on thick. "That nigga been fucking around on you for too long" she continued with sincerity. "You deserve better than him girl for real" she finished looking at me seriously. "Yeah I know bitch, but that nigga is the only man I ever been with" I said sadly. I felt like I was about to start crying. "Don't start that crying bullshit Key, that son of a bitch doesn't deserve your tears baby girl" she stated solemnly.

For the next several days we put in applications and passed out our resumes. That Justin bastard acted like I didn't really matter. He called me maybe twice after I told him it was over. That's that bullshit that I don't like. His punk ass supposed to be blowing up my phone begging for my forgiveness. I guess he really does have a new girl. Damn! Just like that after all these years. I can't even lie to yawl that shit hurt me all the way down into my soul. Have you ever felt that sick feeling in your chest and gut? Couldn't eat, or sleep, or really drink anything. I was just sick with grief. How am I supposed to move on? This mother fucker has broken my heart. I need to find out who this bitch is. I will fuck that little bitch up. Kenia and I started stalking Justin's apartment waiting to find out something. I had me an aluminum baseball bat just in case this shit jumps off. I may split Justin's head wide open for fucking me over like this. Just then we see his car pulling up, and he wasn't alone either. "He got the little bitch with him Key" Kenia whispered. Even though we were in the car with the windows up, and darkly tinted at that, she was still whispering. After he parked, I jumped out the car to confront him and his new bitch. This bastard was walking around the car to open the bitch's door for her. Aww hell no he didn't, that asshole never did that shit for me. As I got closer, he must have heard or sensed something because he turned around suddenly. "So this your little bi…." I began to shout. The sight of her swollen belly as she got up out of the car silenced me. I never expected that. "Key don't start no shit" he said cautiously. "Look we have moved on. You left me remember?" he continued.

I just turned and walked away. The tears were flowing hard and I didn't want him or his bitch to see me like that. I had been trying to get pregnant by Justin for the last two or three years with no luck. Maybe that's why he left me. I couldn't give him a baby so he was moving on. I was even sicker now than I was before, he really hurt me badly with this shit. I thought of all the things we had been through. He taught me how to kiss, how to fuck, how to suck his dick until he came in my mouth. At first, I hated sucking his dick, but he liked it so much that I learned to like it for him. Everything that I know about sex and relationships I learned from him. What was I going to do now? I gave him my best years. My teens and the start of my twenties. I felt like I was getting old. I wanted to start my family before I got too old. I wanted to have a baby before I turned 30. "Ok Justin" I thought to myself. "Fuck you too mother fucker" I mumbled under my breath. For the next several days I wallowed in my pain, contemplated suicide, and laid around my mom's house looking bad, feeling bad, and even smelling bad. I felt so sick that I just wanted to die. My girl Kenia stayed by my side through it all. She cried with me and kept me from hurting myself. I love that bitch with everything that I am.

We finally got called for a security job at this food warehouse. "Top flight security!" we joked after our interview. We were scheduled together so we rode together, and that made it easier. As the weeks passed, I wasn't hurting as bad as I was before. I had even thought about flirting with this good-looking guy at the job. He worked in the factory as maintenance or something I'm not sure. I really didn't care either. Almost every girl on the security team talked about him. Fuck that shit I'm getting that man before one of these stank bitches beats me to it. When I was doing my walk around, I saw him approaching with another guy. "Hi handsome" I said to him coyly. "Hello there" he stuttered. As I walked by, I turned to see if he looked back. YES! He was looking at my butt as I walked away. That was a good sign because I know I had a nice ass. The guard uniform pants fit me just right. Later that day here he comes out to the guard shack. Kenia and I glanced at each other quickly before he walked in. "Hello ladies" he said smoothly.

"I received a complaint about your bathroom?" he continued. "Dang! About time somebody came to fix it. It's been almost two weeks" I said dryly. I walked past him into the bathroom to give him another glimpse of this ass and to show him the problem.

That was how it began between Robert and me. It was so sweet and innocent in the beginning. He was a true gentleman, and he took me out to eat regularly. We went to the movies, walks in the park. And he was ten years older than Justin, but you wouldn't know it from looking at him. The first time we made love I was so nervous. I wanted him badly but I had never been with anyone besides Justin. It went smoothly though. This old man could go. We would do it all over my mom's house. All over his house. In the car in the park, we did it everywhere. When I gave him some head he was shaking and shivering so much that I was turned on. And oh my goodness his head game was unreal. Needless to say, I had put Justin out of my mind. It was perfect. Then out of nowhere Justin showed up over my mom's house. I wondered how he even knew that I was at my mom's or was it just a coincidence? I just looked at him like he was batshit crazy. "Boy what the fuck do you want?" I asked him rudely. "Just stopped by to see how you was doing" he replied smiling stupidly. "I'm doing great baby boy. Better than I ever have before." I replied with a smirk on my face. Before he could even speak again, I rudely asked him to leave. "Don't ever come back Justin" I told him sincerely. "We have moved on remember?" I continued. "Ok take care Kierra" he replied sheepishly as he turned to leave.

As the days passed by, I was loving Robert more and more. I had never prayed for anything before, but I thanked God for bringing us together. After only fucking with Robert for a few weeks I got pregnant. It was really kind of fucked up because the timing of it all made me think that it could be either one of these guys' kid. I had been fucking Justin raw for years and never once got prego. This veteran done put that grown man dick on me and put a child in me too. I had been wanting to have a baby for some time now and was beginning to think that I couldn't have kids. I looked up and thanked God again. At this rate I was going to be up in somebody church. I was so happy to be finally about to have a baby. I just didn't want to be all old and shit bringing my family up. To me if I wouldn't have gotten pregnant before I was like 27 or 28 then it was over. In my mind once you get over 25 you getting old as a female. Men on the other hand only get better with age. Men are wiser and kinder the older they get. They are more responsible the older they get. That's exactly why I hooked up with Justin in the first place. Dudes my age were just not at all appealing. Playing games, thinking they players, and the worst thing of all was that young dudes were broke. No car, no place of their own, no class. It was just a no brainer for me.

Robert was definitely an upgrade from Justin. He just had way more polish than Justin. He was calm and mature and he treated me like his queen. He opened up doors, he bought me nice things without me asking him to. I started thinking that marriage was in the cards for Robert and I. When I told him that I was pregnant he looked surprised then happy. "Baby we are having a baby?" he whispered in my ear as he hugged me and kissed me. I moved in with Robert and we made plans for our future. We picked out our babies' things together. We painted the baby's room with bright neutral colors since we didn't know the sex yet but were intent on having everything fresh and new regardless. My life was going so well that I really started saying thank yous to god several times each day. I am telling yawl that I never ever prayed before now. NEVER. I wasn't raised in the church but Robert was and he would say his grace before each meal. He would kneel beside our bed and pray before going to bed each night. I asked him what he prayed for one day and he said he no longer prayed for anything. "So why you kneeling on the side of our bed for every night?" I asked him sarcastically. He looked me in the face and told me that he had received his blessing in me and that every night he thanked God for bringing me to him. I gave that man some super head that night.

My name is Robert Watson and I am a 42-year-old single black man. I am single because I have had bad luck with the ladies. The simple fact being that I just don't know how to pick em. Since I am being given this opportunity to tell my side of this story let me be completely honest about everything. The women I have been with are not to blame; I am. I have been fortunate in my time to have always had a selection of ladies. This has caused me to be an asshole of sorts. My goal was to bone and after I boned then I was on to the next. I had a strict two bone maximum clause in my player handbook credentials. From experience

I have learned that most women can be boned a maximum of 2 times before they start catching feelings. There are of course exceptions to every rule, but for the sake of this story we will keep it all really simple. For the most part you can get away with a one-night stand 99 percent of the time. Boning twice brings your chances of getting away unscathed down to about 75 percent. If you dip three times then you are almost certain to get crazy bitch shit once you try to get away. Don't take my word for it fellas do your own research. All that being said I take full responsibility for my failed relationships. For some odd reason the few times that the two-bone rule was violated I would try to make the relationship work. And each time it would not work out. The absolute definition of insanity.

It is extremely difficult to navigate relationship waters. Even if you're a professional sailor such as myself, the murky waters of male and female relations can cause even the most experienced sailor to hit rock or ice berg. Before I had met Kierra, I had sworn that I was done with relationships. I was strictly on some bone once, twice at the most, and done shit. The last situation I was in before Kierra had me in the straight up captain save a hoe category. Something about the head, or the pussy had my dumb ass sprung. It was a true out of body experience for me because I was watching from outside myself as I was being played and I could do nothing to stop it. That made me go back to my old playboy self until I met Kierra. This bitch came out of left field for real. I had just been working a new job for a few weeks when she caught my eye. I was maintenance at a distribution warehouse and she was security. I wasn't even on no bitches at all until one day she walked by speaking to me. Instantly it was like I was asleep and awoke to a vision of her. I never bought into that love at first sight shit until that moment. As I watched her fine ass walk past me, I knew that I wanted that woman. The plot began. How could I get this beautiful woman to let me take her out? I could tell that she was younger than me but I wanted her non the less.

I began to make excuses to visit the guard shack. And every time I went out there, I tried to flirt with Kierra. She would flirt back too but I was still apprehensive because of our age difference. She broke the ice by inviting me out to eat with her. I was flabbergasted to say the least. I just could not believe my good fortune. Even if this never worked out at least I had the chance to shoot my shot. Having her all to myself without all those creepy bitches that worked in the guard shack was a blessing sent from God himself. It was hard to try to be subtle about shooting it to a female when there were obstacles called hating ass bitches all in the mix. On Kierra's days off the other bitches would make maintenance requests to make me go out there and listen to their bullshit. "Boy fuck Kierra she has a man already. I will put this pussy and mouth on you like nobody ever has" said one of the haters. Now mind you that I never ever received this kind of attention before. It was only after I started pursuing Kierra that now all of a sudden, I'm a hot boy. I can't lie I did end up sliding up in one of them, but she was an OG and knew how to be discreet. If I would have fucked one of those young bitches Kierra's age then it would have been broadcast all over the whole warehouse.

I tried to play the super gentleman's role but the truth was that I was nervous on how to seal the deal. I had never messed around with anyone half my age and it made me shaky I guess you could say. She practically forced me to get up in that ass after we had gone out for drinks and some late-night food. She took me to a park overlooking the city sky line. We walked around holding hands talking and laughing and then she went down on me in the park. Don't get me wrong I have had many women give me head, but it was something about the way she was doing it that fucked my head all the way up. I came in her mouth and she would not stop until I almost punched her. I was shook and it was a wonderful feeling. Very rarely will a woman give you some head before you fuck her. That shit just doesn't happen very often. My whole intention after that was to give her as good as she had given me. I got my chance a couple days later when she stayed the night with me. Once I spread her legs apart and put my head between those creamy thighs I went to work. I was licking and kissing and sucking her pussy slowly then faster then slowly again until I began to taste her sweetness. She began to try to push my face away but I was stronger than her. I made her take it until she collapsed in exhausted relief.

I really hate to dwell on the sexual parts of how we fell in love but facts are facts. Her freakiness took me to a place I had never been and that made everything else possible. I wanted to do everything for this girl but she wouldn't let me. She would spoil me to the extreme. She would take me shopping. ME SHOPPING? Yeah it was incredulous but it made me know that she really loved me. So many women want a man to spend on them while they just take it and brag to their friends like girl, he bought me this and he bought me that. My baby Kierra was different. We never argued at all. It was just all love all the time. She wasn't no miserable ass bitch either. Always complaining about her ex, always mad, always hard to please. No, my baby was just as happy as I was. She took me to one of her family functions and to be honest I really didn't know what to expect. But it was cool except for one cousin of hers. This bitch ass nigga acted like he had a crush on his own blood. Making stupid ass comments about some nigga named Justin. He was definitely weird as fuck but he didn't spoil our fun. Her granddad was one of the coolest dudes I have ever had the pleasure of meeting. We chopped it up for a long time. He explained to me how Kierra was just like his very own daughter even though she was his granddaughter. He just wanted to make sure that I was about the right thing when it came to Kierra. Her moms was my age but she was still cool and to be honest under different circumstances I would have slid her fine ass. The overall feeling that I got from her family function was that they were all fairly close and loving. But her granddad ran shit for real.

While we were driving home, I had to sort of babysit Kierra. She was not a drinker but she had been drinking like a motherfucker at the get together. She made me pull over so she could pee on the side of the highway. She threw up crying telling me how much she loved me. She cried and confessed the whole ride home. If you didn't know before, now you know that a drunk woman crying and talking is her true to life confessions. All my baby kept telling me was how glad she was that we had met and how much she loved me. I got her home and laid her down to sleep it off. I laughed to myself at the entire night before falling asleep beside her. When I woke up, she was still snoring loudly. I thought that was so cute. Of course I recorded her snoring so that I would have proof. No woman admits to snoring they just talk about you and your snoring. I made us breakfast and let my baby have her breakfast in bed. She fought waking up but I insisted that she eat something. After we ate, we started talking about the night before and we laughed at her condition. "Baby you are not a drinker" I told her laughing. She shook her head in agreement between snorkels of laughter. During those days we had such fun together. I really enjoyed those days more than any other days of my life up to that point. It was like she had breathed fresh life into me. I had sworn to not get involved any more but Kierra came along and changed all of that.

Everything between Kierra and me was going so well that I started to consider how I was going to propose marriage to her. I stayed prayed up and I was thanking God for this woman every day. When she told me that she was pregnant I was shocked and apprehensive at the same time. I mean don't get me wrong I truly loved this woman, but for some reason all of the things that people would have to say crossed my mind. "You too damn old to be having babies", "That girl too young for you" etc. etc. etc. Then just as quickly I eliminated those thoughts and said to myself "Fuck what anybody has to say" I pay my own way. I'm happy so that's all that matters. I wanted us to have a happy family and I wasn't going to let opinions get into our relationship. All of that changed in the blink of an eye. I wanted to surprise my baby so I came home early and saw her getting into a strange car. I really didn't think anything of it I figured it was one of her friends or whatever. I wanted to see how long she was going to be gone though because I wanted us to go out to eat so I flagged the car down. A dude gets out of the car and approaches my window. "Me and Kierra have some unfinished business pops" he said. I put the car in park so I could get out and see for myself. Kierra jumped out screaming "Please no drama. PLEASE!". I was stunned. She ushered the dude back into the car before returning to my window. "This is my ex baby. Me and him need to talk. I will see you later" she told me all of that without looking me in my face. Then she went and got back into his car and they drove off. I have never felt so crushed in my life.

Kierra didn't come back that night, or the next night. She just left me there feeling stupid as fuck heart broken. She had movers and her mother come to get her things from my place. Her mom hugged me and said her goodbyes. Her sad eyes told me exactly what I wanted to deny, but that I had to come to accept as my new reality. At the snap of a finger my life was in shambles. I couldn't talk to anyone about this because the opinions would start again. "Well what do you expect from a young girl?", "She was way too young for you anyway" etc. etc. etc. I was beyond pissed this was just unbelievable. What about our baby? Was that bitch really this heartless? For the next few weeks, I stayed pretty buzzed up. I went through a few one nighters to take off the edge. I was not going to be in pain and blue balled at the same time. Fuck that shit! Didn't someone say that the best way to get over a bitch is to get up inside of another one? So one nighters it was. I left my job because it was too embarrassing and painful there now. I found another gig across town where I was unknown and determined to keep it that way. I could never be gay but because of her I was on some real fuck a bitch shit, word to Biggie. Back to my two hitter quitter rules. Back to concentrating on work. I had a nice career and I made decent money. Hell, this new job payed better but it was third shift which was the only drawback. I began to pray for my sanity and I asked God to send me a Godly woman or leave me to my own devices and whoring. I tried to forget all about Kierra and her being pregnant but in the back of my mind she remained like residual smoke. Refusing to dissipate, refusing to be blown away so easily. Preferring to linger in the dark corners of my mind like a foul odor.

Justin has been bugging the shit out of me all of a sudden. After ignoring his annoying ass for days, I finally decide to answer his call and see what the hell he wanted. He was crying and hysterical on the phone I could barely understand what he was saying. Some shit about his baby and we were always meant to be. I told the damn fool that I would meet him at my mom's house later that day. Robert worked third shift and I wanted to make sure my present didn't get ruined by my past. Robert and I were happy and I was certain that he loved me. My mom and my sister Sydney didn't like Robert though. "Girl that old nigga probably got bitches everywhere and kids", "You and Justin have history girl don't throw that away for some old motherfucker that you will have to wipe his ass soon", they poured it on and on and on. It all made me think was I really in love with Robert or was this relationship just some rebound shit? I still held feelings for Justin but he had done me so wrong. Robert had been so kind to me, so sweet to me, I felt like a piece of shit for even having these thoughts. And what about my baby? My mind was scrambled at the moment. If I would have been in my right mind, I wouldn't have even cared about whatever the fuck Justin was going through. I should have said fuck him just like he said fuck me.

He was already at my mom's house when I arrived pacing back and forth on the porch like a crazed bull. "What's up Justin? It's late and I'm tired" I told him agitated. He began to explain how sorry he was about everything and that he was sure that the baby in my belly was his. He got down on one knee begging me to take him back. He grabbed ahold of my hands and looked at me pleading his case. Then he pulled a ring box out and opened it. "Please Key. Be my wife. Fuck that old ass bastard. We have years together baby not just a few months". I began to cry from all of this and I had to sit down. We entered the house and sat down on the couch. This was just too much. I asked him about the other girl and the baby. He looked down at the floor before mumbling that the baby wasn't his. Wow so that's what this was all about he had been played by the little bitch he played me for. "I have a man now Justin and…" he interrupted my words with a passionate kiss. I half-heartedly tried to push him away but I soon melted into his arms. We ended up making love that night before I shamefully went to Robert's place. What have I done? What will I do? I loved them both but Justin and I do have a bond that is unlike anything I can describe.

We continued the creep moves for a few days. I just didn't know how to break it off with Robert or even if I really wanted to. Robert came home from work early one night busting me and Justin together. "Oh my God" was all that I could say. Justin got out of the car to confront Robert and I couldn't stand for either of them to be hurt so I jumped out the car to diffuse the situation and let Robert know that I would talk to him later. I couldn't even look at him but I could tell that he was hurting badly. Tears flowed from my eyes as we pulled away because I knew that there was no going back to that wonderful man and it was painful. Justin was happy and he treated me so nice for the next several days. He booked us a getaway to Las Vegas for a few days. Even though I loved Justin a whole lot the thoughts and feelings that I had for Robert were still in my heart. I wondered how he was doing and how he was getting along. I wondered if he hated me. If he did, I deserved it. The days turned to weeks and the weeks into months and my baby girl was born on August 12th. The baby looked like Justin I guess or did she look like Robert? To be honest I couldn't tell because they both sorta kinda favored each other. What can I say? I like my man a certain way. I asked Justin if he wanted to do DNA. He refused and signed my baby's birth certificate.

The feeling that my baby was Robert's never left me, but Justin took being a dad very seriously. I reasoned that as long as my baby had love then it was all good. My love for Justin was much deeper and more profound than what I felt for Robert. I felt bad for how I treated him, but like my sister said" Get him before he gets you girl. These niggas aint loyal". So that was that. Justin and I were engaged to be married and our baby was happy and healthy, life was good. One night Justin asked me if I wanted to have another baby. He caught me off guard with that question even though the thought had crossed my mind. I told him if he wanted another baby then we could do it. He looked away from me while he explained that he couldn't make babies. His sperm count was next to zero and the surgery to repair his system was very expensive. "Can you get the old guy to put another baby in you?" he asked me seriously. "Me and him could pass for relatives so it's perfect. Look at Desi" he stated with conviction. I was dumbfounded to say the least. I thought about what he was saying though. "Justin you have known all this time that Desi is not your child?" I asked him. "Baby I love you and I love Desi. I love our family. My dream has always been to have two kids with you and live our lives together" he spoke humbly and sincere. "I know that you have always wanted to be a mother just like I have always wanted to be a father. It doesn't matter where the sperm comes from it only matters that we raise our family in love and keep this between us to the grave" he finished. I told him that I would think about it.

I thought long and hard about it and I really did want another child. And I did want my children to have the same father. I just couldn't find a way to tell Robert what I wanted. He probably hates my guts after what I put him through. Justin was right about our baby girl though. She was so beautiful and charming. If this was what we were going to do then Robert was the obvious choice. I knew for a fact that he had strong feelings for me, and I really thought that I felt the same for him. I reasoned that everything happens for a reason and our reason for meeting each other was for him to give me my children. So I reached out to him. I decided to just be straight up with him fuck all the bullshit. This was real life and I needed his sperm. I left him several messages before he finally responded back to me. His voice was cold and distant. He didn't want to talk to me and it was very obvious. He asked me what I wanted, so I explained what I wanted from him. I left out the part about Justin making the request. "Just give me another child Robert and I will never bother you again" I told him. He hung up the phone and it was three or four days before I heard from him again. During those days I was sending him naked pictures of me. Text messages begging him to put his dick in my mouth. I was desperate dammit. So I made up my mind to do whatever it took.

My life was just starting to get back into a normal swing when out of left field this bitch Kierra is calling me and texting me again. I couldn't even imagine what the hell she could want from me after the way things went before. All of the feelings that I thought were dead reemerged inside of me and that sick feeling returned in earnest. "This bitch is the devil" I reasoned to myself. Why else would she continue to torture me after the humiliating treatment she gave me before? I had me a couple little broads that were content to bone somewhat regularly while I sorted my life out. That's the excuse that I gave them when they spoke of a relationship. Well the storm has returned I thought. She must want some money or something for the baby was the reasoning I used to answer her call. Well I really thought that I had heard it all, but when this crazy bitch asked me to give her another baby, she took the cake. I hung up on her stupid ass. The next few days she just would not let up. Every day I was getting pictures, texts, and all manner of sexual inuendo from her. The thought of having sex with her again was very tempting, but when she started talking about giving me that mouthpiece again, I knew that I was going to give in. That girl's head game is unlike any other. She used to suck me while I drove down the street or on the highway, and she always made me cum. After she made me cum, she would not stop she would keep going and going driving me crazy in the process.

My dumb ass ended up going to see just what this bitch Kierra wanted. I tried to reason that it was curiosity and I just wanted the bitch to leave me alone. Honestly, I was simply flat out in love with her. There has never been a woman that made me feel that way. I could try and tell yawl it was all about the sex because she was a freak for sure, but it was more than that and I am incapable of describing it exactly. Is this the love that I have been hearing about my whole life? All the songs, movies, and books that have been written about love made me wonder if this was in fact my unicorn. If this is my unicorn then that is so fucked up. Or maybe I just can't accept the fact that she chose him over me. Maybe some man ego thing deep within me hates to lose. And it was in fact a loss I have to admit it. Why did my love have to be consumed with a no-good liar like Key? The joke is obviously on me. When I pulled up to get her, I watched as she approached and the stirrings began in my loins. I felt excited and disappointed at the same time. She opened the door and slid into the passenger seat of my car looking and smelling like heaven. I may have started drooling I don't remember, but she got in and straight reached for my dick. She grabbed it and rubbed it and the whole time I'm just staring at her like a fucking nut case. After I felt myself getting hard, I pushed her hand away. The spell momentarily broken. Undaunted she reached for my pants and started unfastening them to pull them down. "Chill the fuck out! Damn!" I yelled at her.

I began to drive and I was sweating now. This bitch pushed a button inside of me that turned me on so much it was incredible. 0 to 100 real real quick. I was so hard at this point that it was painful. My manhood needed to escape the confines of my draws and my pants. She reached over to finish removing my pants as I drove. I didn't even try to stop her this time. She had them down around my ankles like magic and then the magic began when she put me into her soft, wet mouth. She caressed me with her lips and her tongue bringing me to the brink almost instantly. She could tell though so she altered her method so I wouldn't cum just yet. My entire body was shaking so violently that I had to pull the car over before I killed us both. Then she let me cum into her willing mouth drinking all of my juices until I was dry. I had to push her head away because she was not going to stop. I put my head back on the headrest and closed my eyes for a moment. That shit right there is why this bitch is so dangerous I thought to myself. I opened my eyes and looked over at her and she was watching me. "What?" I asked her. "Nothing just looking at you" she replied. "Did you like that?" She asked me. "What do you think?" I responded. She knew that that shit was fire. And me cumming in like 3 minutes was the evidence.

After we rode for a while making small talk, she finally asked me if I would do it? She wanted me to give her my seed for her and her man to raise as their own. We went to the park and we walked and we talked and she explained that she never meant to hurt me but she really loved Justin. The only thing was that Justin couldn't make a baby. I want both of my babies by the same man she told me seriously. I will never ask you for anything Robert. If you do this for me, I will be forever grateful. She was pouring it on thick and after that fire ass mic check? I would have done just about any damn thing she asked me to do. So I agreed and we proceeded to my house to start the process. We fucked into the wee hours of the next day. Stopping for recovery and sustenance. She was a master at her craft the pleasure that I was experiencing was indescribable. I ended up cumming three more times before she left. I fell into a deep coma like sleep, not waking up until early afternoon. I felt so good, so alive, so happy. I wish that I could bottle up the sex that Key has. Bottle it and manufacture that shit. I would be the richest man on this planet. I went about the rest of my day floating on cloud nine.

Key called me again three days later telling me that she wanted to have another session to make sure the process worked. She reasoned that we may have to do it several times before it actually worked. I was game for that shit. Hell, I was downright giddy about the notion of fucking this girl again no matter the reason. I informed her that it might be better if we just hung out for a couple weeks fucking every day just to be sure she got the result she wanted. She laughed at that, but replied no. She was fine with us boning regularly like this until she was pregnant. I was cool getting what I was getting anyway, but I still wanted to see how far I could push her. Over the next couple weeks, we were like rabbits. We did it everywhere. Mall restrooms, movie theater restrooms, in the car, at her mom's house. We even did it at her and Justin's place when he was at work. In the shower, on their bed, on their couch, in the kitchen. I would think about what would happen if he came home early one day and I was all up inside Key. Would he have a sucker attack? Would he try to knuckle up? Would he try to kill me? I kept my pistol with me just in case. I was hoping that she would never get pregnant and we could just keep on fucking like this forever. Reality slapped me in the face because she called me with the good news that she was pregnant. Don't worry she told me we can still keep fucking for as long as you want. I wonder if she could feel how hard I was cheesing on this end of the phone.

Robert took forever to respond back to me, but just as soon as he did, I knew that he was going to do it. For one reason or another this man truly cared for me. Sure, he would play hard because of his pride but in the end his heart belonged to me. I'm not trying to come off as cocky or anything just stating facts. Him and I have a connection that is almost palpable. I am in love with Justin, but I am also in love with Robert. The love I feel for each man is different though. Justin has been around me for so long that we are like really good friends as well as lovers. I know his ways, his habits, his likes and dislikes. He is the man that I want to spend the rest of my life with, but then there's Robert. I blame Justin for it because if he would have been acting right me and Robert would have never even met. The sex with Robert is unreal. He takes such pleasure in everything that I do to him. He gets so turned on that it turns me on even more. His entire body be shaking when I top him off. That shit makes my pussy so fucking wet that I just be fiending for him to get inside of me. Justin gave me the green light to fuck him so I planned to keep on fucking him. Fuck it I will keep both of these niggas all to myself. If one of them gets mad or gets with another bitch I'm cutting his ass off and keeping who's left.

I talked a real tough game but to be honest it was going to hurt me if I lost either one of my dudes. I guess you could pretty much label our situation messy as fuck, but I didn't ask for this shit to fall into my lap. I couldn't have mapped this shit out in a million years even if I tried. Sometimes life has a strange way of testing you, and I couldn't tell you whether I was passing my test or failing it. What I can tell you is that this shit feels good and I don't want nothing about it to change. Since I was pregnant again Justin told me that he expected me to stop fucking around with Robert. I just shook my head like yeah ok whatever nigga. I was not going to stop fucking that man until he gets tired of me and moves on. Like I said, I love Justin but he needs to stay in his fucking lane. Worrying about what Rob and I do is only going to hurt his feelings. Besides, what he doesn't know can't hurt him I reasoned.

Robert has given me another baby. Our first baby girl is just so precious, so pretty, and so smart. Hopefully this one will be a boy. I wondered if Justin would be ok with us naming him Robert. Shit Justin ass would shit a fucking brick if I even mentioned some shit like that. I chuckled to myself at that thought. Life was good and I had nothing to complain about at the moment.

As the weeks rolled by Robert and I kept up our side romance. He even took me to a couple doctor appointments when Justin couldn't make it. The more I was around him the more that I wanted to be around him. I began to wonder if we could all just share a home together. They could be brother husbands or some shit. That thought cracked me up and I laughed out loud. Robert looked over at me like I was crazy. I was happy as can be when Robert crushed my happy thoughts all of a sudden. "I can't do this anymore. I won't do this anymore Key" he remarked slowly. He was saying every word slowly and deliberately. He sounded so cold and detached. I wondered how long he had been feeling this way so I asked him that. He explained that even though he loved me, that he could no longer be my fuck boy. I tried to tell him that he was so much more than just my fuck boy, but his mind was made up. He wished me the best and dropped me off. Just like that my life got turned upside down. For the next several days I was downright depressed. Justin thought that it was just my pregnancy fucking with me. I couldn't tell him that my lover had dumped me because of him. I really couldn't blame Rob for how he felt because honestly, I would probably feel the same as he does. So I silently wished Robert a good life and reasoned that I would always have a piece of him close to me. Whenever I get to missing him, I can look at the beautiful children he gave me and smile.

I had had enough of the back and forth with Key. She made me feel so damn good but she also took me to a dark place when I imagined how I really wanted our lives to be. I'm the one who gave her what she wanted. It should be us raising a family together. I needed a drink so I went to the liquor store for some cognac. I went home alone to drink and to think. As the alcohol relaxed me my mind drifted and I thought about each happy moment that I could remember with Key. The good times were always accompanied by mind blowing sex sessions. I began to be honest with myself as I realized and admitted that this had to be

God's plan. She wanted him in her life not me. Since he was incapable of making a baby God blessed them with my seed. It was really bugging me that we were creeping around like criminals. In the beginning I was turned on by the sneaking around, and I wanted to be in her presence no matter what. As time went on and we were spending so much time together I knew that I couldn't share her any longer. Sometimes you have to be real about your feelings to yourself. I love Kierra more than life itself. I love her so much that I had to let her go on with her life. I hope her and Justin will be happy and prosperous.

At work there was a young lady whom had caught my eye. She had the body of a goddess, and she had that dark chocolate complexion that I loved. We had become acquainted on a friendly speaking level before Key and I had hooked back up. I was walking through the cafeteria with my head down mourning the loss of my love when she startled me. "Hey stranger where you been?" she asked me cheerfully. I was so deep in thought that I stuttered, mumbled a reply. "Hi how are you" is what came out. "Wow you have forgotten all about me already?" she stated playfully. Her positive mood and spirit were infectious and my own spirits were lifted as by magic. "Thank you so much" I told her returning her smile. She stared at me confused before asking "For what?" I just shook my head and my hands and told her to forget about it. I joined her on our break and we talked and laughed and connected instantly. After our break was over and I returned to work my spirits were lifted and so was my mood. I was thinking to myself about how nice of a woman Ms. Beverly was. She certainly appeared to be the total package. She was beautiful, in tip top shape, amazing body, enlightened personality, intelligent and funny conversation. I could go on but you get the point. I was thoroughly impressed by Beverly. But let me pump my brakes dammit.

I was determined to be cautious with Beverly, because it seemed like she was feeling me, and I could not take another episode of love then loss. Fuck that shit that shit hurt. BAD! You feel me? Well if your reading this then let me wish you the best and that you never have to feel what I felt when my heart was broken into pieces. I was nervous and pessimistic; it was just too damn good to be true. After you have had your heart and soul crushed by misgiven love it is extremely difficult to open yourself back up. My antennas were up, I was looking for any excuse to run away. Beverly never gave me an excuse though; she was quite literally perfect. There were no crazy exes or baby daddies. She had no children, but she had an ex that had treated her badly. We shared that misfortune, and perhaps that's why we bonded the way we did. We clicked on a deep level that was beyond lust and sex. I was shocked at this turn of events. My optimism grew with each moment we shared. This woman was perfect. She was my unicorn. After the hell that was Kierra this was such a welcome circumstance. I looked to the heavens as I am want to do, and I thanked God for bringing her to me. My life had changed for the better despite me and my stupidity. I had no choice but to thank my father in heaven for smiling on me once again. God's love truly knows no bounds.

Several months have passed and I find myself not thinking about Key hardly at all. I was happy with my life with Beverly. My career had skyrocketed and we were expecting a little boy soon. To be perfectly honest I never thought that my life would take this kind of turn. My salary had increased mightily. I had never dreamed of making this type of money. I proposed to Beverly at the baby shower and she accepted making me the happiest man on earth. There were moments when I would still question what I did to deserve such a great woman as Beverly. I guess I will forever possess a certain pessimism within me no matter what even though I pray for God to release me from it. Happy days overwhelmed me with Beverly. She catered to my every wish, my every need without any complaints. Whenever the thought of Key and the two children we made together came to my mind a profound melancholy would subdue me. I became an alcoholic. I functioned normally, I still went to work, I still handled my business and payed my bills. But I drank liquor almost every day. As soon as work was done, I had a cup in my hand. Now don't get me wrong I have for my entire adult life been a drinker. But I never drank every day. If this was the price I had to pay for letting Kierra into my life then so be it. I focused on making Beverly happy. Life goes on.

The blessings were raining down on Beverly and me, I was making money in my sleep and my baby was getting promotions as well. We bought matching vehicles; we purchased several acres of land to build our home on. As our home was being built, I received more promotions and offers to make myself into THE premier area manager. I was to run the entire east coast. Warehouses located from Maine to Florida. It was a huge responsibility and a tremendous wage increase. We couldn't be happier. Our baby boy was born on a sunny afternoon after having his mom in labor for almost 17 hours. I told Beverly that her pussy was so damn good that the boy didn't want to come out of it. "He just like his daddy" she quipped back at me. He was a beautiful, healthy baby boy. I said a prayer of gratitude to God. I kissed Bev and thanked her as well for doing such a good job. Later that day I hooked up with my brother and we drank a toast to my new son. We laughed and talked about days past. I was happy and I knew that I was blessed.

Three years later Justin and I are happily married, our kids Desi and JJ were four and three respectively. I still think of Robert of course from time to time. It's kind of hard not to with both of his children running around my house looking just like that nigga. But I am happy with Justin. He has stepped up and been a great father to our babies. He doesn't cheat on me anymore. Or if he does, he has gotten super slick with it. He never stays out all night anymore. He has truly manned up and I am happy and proud to have him as my husband. Our lives were moving along nicely before Justin got into a bad car accident. To be honest I didn't think the fender bender was all that when I first got the call. As the days went by afterward things were scary and crazy at the same time. Our income was already not really all that, but with Justin unable to work the economic pressure was palpable. His condition prevented him from continuing with the job he had been doing since high school. He had to lose one of his legs. His insurance only paid so much and only for a limited amount of time. We needed to reevaluate our financial situation asap.

The thought to call Robert never even crossed my mind. My sister brought up his name after Justin's injury. "Girl you need to call your kid's real daddy now!" she quipped. Robert had given me any and everything that I had ever asked of him. And that's despite the way that I have dogged him throughout our time knowing each other. There was absolutely no way that I could bring myself to reach out to him now. It just wasn't right no matter how you looked at it. Yes, we both knew that both of my babies were in fact his babies, but Justin had signed both birth certificates. His life insurance named our kids in it. I had secretly been keeping tabs on Robert. He was doing quite well, him and his little wife. And I congratulated him for doing well, but at the same time I wondered what our lives would have been had I not chosen Justin over him. I realize that now is not the time to be having all of these thoughts about "what if?" scenarios. Nevertheless, here I was having feelings and thoughts of regret. I wondered if Robert would still fuck me the way he used to. Whew chile that man could fuck good! Looking at my babies made me think of him even more. Let me stop with these thoughts right fucking now I scolded myself. I made my bed so now I have to lie in this bed of sadness and regret. Robert deserves to live his life. I could have easily stayed with that man when I had him. Since I had decided to let him go, I had to stick with that decision.

The weeks and the months passed by slowly, and sadly. I busied myself with my baby's lives trying to keep it all together for them. Justin had turned into a whiny, always complaining, alcoholic ass bitch. Lord this man gets on my every nerve. Sometimes the sight of him would just make me sick to my stomach. Still I just wanted my kids to have the best opportunity at a good life that was possible. I had to stop concerning myself with Justin. My sister would not fucking let up about Robert. She had discovered where he lived with his wife and their child. She knew where he worked. "That nigga run shit up in that plant girl" she told me one day. My niece and nephew deserve to have their daddy in their life girl. You and Justin did this weird ass white people shit in the first place. I warned you about it in the beginning but you never fucking listen. Now here you are looking pitiful every damn day. With that sorry motherfucker Justin feeling sorry for himself, just giving up on life. Drinking all day every day. Desi and Justin Jr are still very young and they really do need their real father in their lives. Are you going to let your pride or some fucked up sense of doing the right thing keep the best life away from your kids? My sister just would not let up. "Bitch you and mom were the ones always telling me to leave Robert alone. He was too old, or he was this or he was that. Fuck your opinion or anybody else opinion. Mind your own heffa" I shouted to my sister. "The right thing would have been to never have children with one man and let another man claim them as his. Key that shit is the devil" she was preaching now. I was relieved when she finally left. She is right of course but the truth hurts especially when you have been telling yourself the exact same shit. I didn't know what I was going to do at the moment, so I decided to think about everything before making a final decision.

"Mr. Watson there is a young lady here to see you" my secretary informed me. "Ok send her in Angie please and thank you" I responded. In walks Kierra's sister Sydney with a serious look on her face. I say to her "how may I help you?" with a forced smile on my face. She explained to me how things were going for Kierra and the children that I had fathered. She explained that she was concerned for the wellbeing of her niece and nephew. I listened politely and without interruption even though I wanted to put her out of my office. "You are their father Robert. They know and love Justin as their dad, but you are the real dad. You and Justin should work out how yawl are going to deal with this" she told me calmly. "I can appreciate your concern Sydney, I really can, but I'm not about to share any children" I told her calmly. "I shared your sister with that nigga, but I be damn if I share some fucking kids" I continued growing angry. "She made the choice. Not me. She chose him. Not me" I continued voice rising. "I have given all that I will give. Now please leave. I don't want to hear anything more that you have to say" I finished calmly. She stared at me with malice for several seconds before speaking venomously "You stupid motherfucker what the fuck did you think would happen? In your simple little mind did you imagine the children you made would never come back to you?" I stood up and walked out of my office leaving her there seething.

The next several days I contemplated everything she had said. I had to admit to myself that this was indeed some messy fucking shit. I had established an entire life with my wife without any thought towards Kierra or Justin or the children. In my mind she and they had gotten what they wanted and moved on with their lives, so I moved on with mine. I was happy with my life the way it was without Kierra and all of the bullshit that accompanied her. All of the goals I had imagined achieving with Kierra were surpassed with my wife. There simply was no going back to what we had, there was no return to the feelings we once shared. All of that was over and yet I felt a tinge of guilt. I felt like I was wrong for abandoning my seed, and at the same time I felt like a "Captain save a ho" word ta forty water. This conundrum was unexpected because I thought they would never reach out to me because that's what Key had told me. It began to dawn on me that Kierra was just a selfish bitch that only worried about Kierra. At the same time, I had to accept my own part in this fiasco. She had told me what was up. I chose to ignore what she said thinking that I could change her mind and win her over. I concluded that this was all my own fault and decided to stand up like the real man that I am.

I reached out to Kierra and let her know how I felt about everything. I explained that I would take over all responsibilities for my children. All that I asked was that she remove Justin as my kids' father. If she was willing to replace his name on my kid's birth certificates with mine then I would pay whatever I had to pay. I just wasn't about to be taking care of my babies and that dead-beat ass dude as well. I knew that it was wrong for me to be feeling animosity towards Justin, but I was straight out jealous of the bond him and Kierra shared even now after all this time has passed. I decided to pray on it and ask God for guidance. Kierra was taking her sweet ass time to get back with me on this new development. It was probably for the best though because I have yet to discuss all of this with my wife. A few days later Kierra responded to my offer in the negative. She told me that she never intended to reach out to me. She explained how her sister needed to stay out of this business. She apologized to me for her sister and all of this mess. I felt like a piece of shit after our conversation. All I was thinking about was myself, my feelings, my jealousy, my hurt pride. I looked at my life and how blessed I have been despite my stupidity. I decided that I would help the family that I helped create get to a better place. I would go home tonight and discuss it all with my better half.

This stupid bitch done went to Robert like it was her place to do so. I was so mad that I wanted to choke the life out of Sydney. She tried to explain to me like she was just concerned. Like she was so fucking worried about my kid's wellbeing. "Bitch you need to have your own fucking kids to worry about. Me and mines are ok" I yelled at her. Instead of choking her I told her to just stay the fuck away from me and my kids. Now Robert sending me some crazy ass shit about putting him on my kid's birth certificates. He must have been high on some powerful drugs to think that I would ever do that. It had a lot more to do with the mental and emotional welfare of my babies than Justin's feelings or Robert's pride. If it came down to it, I could make it without either one of these niggas. I let Robert know how I felt in no uncertain terms. "Just know that I would never come at you like that man" I told him. He was speechless as I told him about Sydney dumbass trying to get all up in our business. I didn't know how to take his silence and I couldn't care less about what he was saying. I went out of my way to be at least somewhat real throughout this crazy ordeal. But fuck the bullshit about me breaking my baby's hearts. Period! They already had a daddy named Justin and that's how it was going to stay.

Sydney had even gone to Justin with the shit and his retarded ass was feeding into it like the sad case he was turning out to be. I was trying my best to be understanding of his dilemma and situation but this nigga was truly pushing it. "Shidd! Fuck that old bastard Key. We could use that money" Justin slurred to me drunkenly. I ignored him and continued doing my baby's hair. He must have picked up on my mood because he suddenly shut the fuck up. It was getting on my nerves how everybody was so hung up on some fucking money without any thought towards how the situation would affect my children. Justin is all that they know. I may be wrong about all of this but I'm not bringing Robert into my kid's lives at this point. Justin can't think past his next drink nowadays. Where does he think it would leave him if I did as he and Robert suggested? Out in the fucking cold, homeless, broke, and now a fucking drunk. He is lucky I love my kids the way I do and that I'm not a money hungry selfish bitch. Even so it is very enticing to leave this fucking struggle shit behind me and live at least a halfway decent life financially. I'm really starting to wonder if continuing on in this dead ass relationship with Justin is even worth it anymore. I have to carry him and my babies by myself. I try to be understanding with him because he has been through a lot, but at this point he seems to have given up on life and himself. That being the case I ask myself what can he offer me and my kids? A hard way to go? A sad case that we have to witness as he kills himself? That is not how I want to raise my kids. I decided right then and there that me and Justin's days in this relationship were numbered. Watching him crumble like this might rub off on my babies. Fuck that shit.

A few days later Robert contacted me and apologized for his behavior and selfishness. He explained that he wanted to make sure that we were alright no matter what. He didn't require me to change my kid's names or status. He said that whatever I needed he would provide. No questions asked. I was overcome with emotion all of a sudden, and I began to sob and cry into the phone. I couldn't help but to wonder about how my life should be right now. This wonderful man was so sweet and understanding. I knew that I was a damn fool to have let him get away from me. After I regained my composure, I told him how grateful that I was for his help. I told him about everything that we had been going through with money problems after Justin's accident. I needed to get it all off of my chest and Robert listened to me quietly without interruption or judgement. After I finished with my whining, he simply asked me what I wanted him to do? I almost started crying again but I kept my cool this time and I told him that we needed a decent place to live first off. "Ok I will call you in a day or two with some prospects" he said simply. Then he politely bid me a good day and got off the phone. I thought to myself that if I ever got another chance with that man that nothing on earth would ever come between us again.

I was feeling good about making the decision to take care of my secret children, but I was nervous about telling my wife. We have never discussed me having other children. I just never saw the need to bring up such a messy situation before now. As I explained the situation to my wife, I could tell that she was not at all pleased. Who could blame her though? She listened to me silently. After I was finished, she sat there quietly for a few moments before responding. "I'm trying to figure out why you have never told me about this before Robert. This was need to know information baby boy" she was speaking calmly with a venomous undertone. "I can hardly believe that the man that I love, the father of my only child, and my husband could have been so fucking stupid" she spat at me words that felt like knives plunging into my heart and soul. "I never signed up for some crazy ass soap opera bullshit Robert. I need some time away from you. I'm really feeling like our marriage has been broken by your naivete, but I will take some time and think this through. In the mean time I want you out of my house pronto!" she finished her response stood up and walked away without a backward glance.

Wow I never expected such a hostile response from Bev. Although it was true that in the grand scheme of things that I should have informed her of the fact that I have outstanding children. It is also a fact that bringing up Kierra and my children with her is an embarrassing proposition. Call me stupid and naïve or whatever but I truly believed that Kierra and everything to do with her was in my past never to be relived again. That's the way I wanted it anyway. Now I'm sick once again. I love my wife and our life and our son, but I feel like I have lost her behind my decision to try and leave the past in the past. Especially when kids are involved. Beverly was a no nonsense straight up real woman whom was above games, lies, and deceit. Right now she was feeling like I had purposely deceived her. At least that's the way I'm taking it. Both her and Sydney had called me stupid for believing that all of this would never come back to haunt me. The fact being that I had done exactly what the woman that I loved had asked me to do. There was no going back now. As painful as losing Beverly was to me, I could not turn my back on my babies no matter what. I was successful, I was indeed a blessed man and there was no possibility of me changing my mind now. At that moment I resigned myself to a live out the twilight of my life alone. I would focus on leaving a legacy for my children and grandchildren.

The next several weeks were very rough on me emotionally and mentally. Beverly had abandoned me totally and filed for divorce. Maybe I was still being naïve but I expected her to at least work out a compromise with me. SOMETHING! But she was hostile and mean towards me at every turn. I tried to reach out to her on several occasions being rebuked at every opportunity. First frustration then anger began to accompany any dealings that we had. I began to call her out of her name whenever we were face to face. I began to resent her inability to understand what I was going through and it made me despise her. Right or wrong these were my feelings. My antagonism towards her fueled her antagonism towards me, and she would frequently cuss me as well. "Nigga your dumb ass fucked up! You having kids all over the damn place without ever telling your wife? Fool fuck you!" she shouted at me after I had referred to her as the bitch from hell. My life had taken a turn towards despair I guess you could say. I prayed on my situation and my lord advised me to man up. I stopped all of the negativity with Beverly, and accepted the consequences of my stupidity. I signed over my rights to the house we had built and got me a condo overlooking the Ohio river. I also bought a condo for Kierra and her family in the same area. It was nice, clean, quiet, and it had an excellent school district.

Just as he had promised Robert called me a few days later with an option to live in a condo in an exclusive neighborhood. He picked me up and let me check out the place. It was absolutely breathtaking with an amazing view of the Ohio river and downtown Cincinnati. It was an extravagant 3-bedroom condo with a 2-car garage. I loved it and he gave me the keys to it and asked if I needed help with furniture and appliances. I told him that we indeed did require assistance. He reached into his wallet and handed me his black card. "Get everything that you need and then return my card to me" he said with a smile. I promise yawl that it took everything inside of me to hold off from dropping to my knees and sucking this man's dick at that moment. It wasn't just how kind he was, or that he was saving me and my babies lives. Ever since we had been back in contact, I was absolutely fiending for his dick. Everything about him had me turned up. The curl of his lips when he talked, the look in his eye, the confident way he walked. I was plotting on Mr. Robert and I wanted it to be perfect this time. I knew that he truly loved his wife and I was not going to disrespect that even though I knew that that bitch couldn't make him feel the way that I made him feel. Justin was a wrap as they say in show business, I think. Regardless of anything he was not moving on with my children and I made it a point to let him know about it.

The next several weeks were hectic to say the least. In between moving and packing and buying new stuff for our new place I had to listen to Justin whine. He expected me to continue the pity party while he drank himself to death or even worse permanently damage the psyche of my children. I wanted my kids to fight through whatever life gives them. Folding is never an option in my book. Yeah life had dealt Justin a cruel blow but he folded and gave up and I didn't want him to be the example my babies learned from every day. We moved into our new place and my babies were so excited and happy. To top it off Robert surprised me again when I returned his card to him. He had taken the trouble of buying us a new vehicle. A brand-new SUV to be exact. He told me that we needed reliable transportation. I started crying again yawl I'm sorry but I just could not help it. I knew in my heart that I did not deserve the kindness that Robert was showing me. I had done him so wrong. The love he was showing me and our babies took over me and I aggressively pulled out his dick and put it in my mouth. Before I could get into really showing him my gratitude, he was cumming down my throat and shaking uncontrollably. I smiled to myself because I still had it.

Over the next few weeks, I gave Robert head about 6 or 7 more times with him busting every time like clockwork. I knew his dick well. He never even tried to resist when I went for his package. He would just let me do whatever I wanted to do. I could have easily fucked him several times, but I wasn't going there just yet. I knew that his wife wasn't satisfying him because my head game had his ass hooked like phonics. I really did want that dick up inside me, but not at the expense of causing him more drama. It was bad enough that I was drinking his semen, but I knew for a fact that once he put his dick back in my pussy, he wasn't going to put it in any other pussy again. EVER! The temptation was almost over whelming but I remained strong. I began to wonder why he was never with his wife. I mean I could understand him not wanting to bring her around us all the time but I have never seen him with the bitch. There aint no fucking way I would be leaving my man alone all the time with a bitch like me. I would be showing up on his arm like "naw bitch I'm wifey stay in your fucking place". This dumb bitch was losing a piece of him every time I put that pretty dick in my mouth. She should thank me for not putting this pussy on him just yet. Her time was running out because I could tell that Robert was wanting to fuck me just as bad as I wanted to fuck him.

When Key had moved in with the kids, I was surprised that her husband wasn't there with them. I wondered about it but I kept my mouth shut, hell I had my own fucked up shit going on. Beverly and I were cordial now, but her love for me had gone away and I felt it just as clearly as a slap to my face. I was very hurt and bitter but I worked through it all trying to be the man that I should have already been. Kierra was helping me keep my sanity because she was topping me off like a champion. It's amazing how good some great head will have you feeling. I mean the world could be ending and you will get that bomb head and be like "Let's get to the next life, the afterlife, shit whatever the fuck they call it just bring that mouth back over here". She was allowing me to see my babies every day. Life that we created together and they were both so beautiful and smart. That nigga could have never made babies so smart and beautiful. He should be thanking me every fucking day he wakes up. Let me stop with the negativity I chided myself. God was continuing to bless me despite my sinful behavior, so I had to try and do better.

Being around Key this much was intoxicating in and of itself but every time she puts her mouth on me it breaks down any and all barriers that I may have been trying to uphold. I could not even play like I was in resistance any more. I dreamed of the day when we would have nasty, sweaty, exhausting sex. I wanted her so bad that my dick stayed semi hard any time that she was around me. I wondered if she knew how I was feeling. I mean Key had a bad ass mouthpiece on her, but she also had an incredibly juicy, delectable, box that always left me wanting more and more. Her sex game had me fucking her like I was still in my twenties. She pushed all the right buttons that brought me to life. There was a time when I couldn't understand why older guys fucked around with women half their age. Now I could feel them. Now I understood that this shit was like the fountain of youth. This bitch had dogged me. Treated me like a piece of trash easily discarded. She had also brought me back to life, back from the dead you might say. How she made me feel when it was on, made up for the pain that I experienced when it was off.

The rollercoaster ride that my life has turned into was exhausting and exhilarating at the same damn time. The pain and disappointment from Beverly tired me out and filled me with regret. While the pleasure and excitement that Kierra provided gave me a rush like really pure cocaine, or 12 shots of espresso for the non-initiated. Regardless of your experiences I just want you to understand the rush this woman gave me. She could keep using me until she used me up. I resigned myself to being pride less when it came to dealing with Kierra. Fuck it! I had not seen her husband not one time since they moved. Not once. Now as you all can tell I'm not the brightest brain by a long shot, but I know a break up when I see one. Key had to have kicked that nigga to the curb. He hasn't been over this way not one time, and she continues to blow my top off on a regular. I was ready to play in the water if you can catch my drift. As badly as I wanted to fuck the shit out of Key, I was also very apprehensive. This girl has crushed my heart and I don't know if I will survive another episode like that. Deep in my heart I knew that she was driving the car and I was along for the ride. If she came and took my dick right this second and sat on top of it there was absolutely nothing that I could do. I belonged to her totally and unconditionally, and as sad as admitting that made me feel it was the simple truth.

As I looked around my new home, I felt so much love and gratitude for Robert. It's not just because he has done so much for me and our children. What made everything so much more special was because he did all of this despite how bad I had treated him. I regretted ever leaving him for Justin. I was so stupid to listen to my dumb ass sister and anybody else who said that Robert was not my soul mate. This man has shown and proved how he truly feels for me. The fucked up thing about all of that was that I already knew how he felt. I already knew what I had. My dumb stupid ass listened to people who had no idea about the man that Robert was. It's such a blessing that I have been given another chance at the love of my life. And I knew now that this man was in fact the love of my life. He is the man that was made for me. His wife was nowhere to be seen and I had tried to be respectful for the sake of Robert. Fuck all of that polite bullshit now. I had made up my mind that Robert and I would begin a new life together without all of the side noise. If he was willing to take me back then I would do anything he wanted. Even if it involved his wife and me working something out. Shidd me and that bitch can be best of friends, or sister wives, or whatever the fuck Robert wanted from us. Honestly I could care less. I have never been with another woman but I would do it for this man.

I was so horny to fuck Robert that I was making a mess in my panties. Under any other circumstance I would have been embarrassed, but nothing that Robert wanted even if he doesn't know that he wants it was too much or embarrassing. Today was the day and Robert was about to get all up in this pussy. My mom has the kids, I had made it a point to be shined up for my baby. Nothing was ever going to come between us again. A knock at my door interrupted my pornographic fantasies about what I wanted to do to Robert. I looked out the peep hole at Justin. Damn this motherfucker has the most fucked up timing. I opened the door and stood there looking at him with disgust written all over my face. "May I come in? Damn Key! Is it like this now?" he stuttered. I let him in still silent because anything that would have come out of my mouth would not have been nice. He started to explain about how sorry he was about his drunken behavior. He told me that he had joined a treatment group to help him stop drinking. He told me how much he missed me and the kids and that he hoped that we could start over again. I listened to everything that he had to say without interruption. After he finished, I spoke slowly looking him in his eyes. I don't want you anymore Justin. After you left me for that bitch that had you thinking she was having your baby I should have never ever come back to you. I regret that mistake each and every day. I gave up on a man that truly loved me for you. You never even appreciated how difficult that move was on me. Well I'm moving forward with my life Justin. I have no time for any more back tracking with your sorry ass. I stood up to let him out because I was done with this conversation.

After losing part of his leg Justin moved about on crutches or a walker. He rarely used the prosthetic limb made for him. Today he was using his walker. He stood up to leave and paused for a moment before speaking vehemently. "It's so fucked up that you are leaving me now Key. It's even more fucked up that you are taking my kids from me too. And all because your old ass trick has a couple bucks?" he was spitting the words out as he moved towards the door. "If I still had my leg would you be doing this? I doubt it bitch! You aint shit for this Kierra. I hope that old bastard gets tired of your good for nothing ass and gets him another young bitch to replace you." he finished talking and was breathing hard. He was preaching to the choir because I had already made my mind up about the direction my children and I were going to take. Once again his weak behavior had opened up the door for Robert to come into my life, only this time I was going to make sure he stayed right here in my heart. If Justin wouldn't have given up and became an alcoholic whiner, we would still be together. And if was a fifth, we would all be drunk or some shit my uncle used to say any time someone said "what if". Call me a soft-hearted bitch or whatever but I truly felt bad about this entire situation. "Look Justin I'm sorry that life has a fucked up way of challenging us all." I said kindly. "We are not meant to be together baby boy. I made the mistake of coming back to you then, but I can't keep making the same mistakes. Robert makes me happy and it has a lot more to do with feelings and emotions than just money." I explained to him softly. He looked me in my eyes as I spoke to him and the tears welled up in his eyes. Then he left without a backwards glance.

I felt bad for Justin I really did but life goes on. We all live and eventually learn one way or another. I had learned that I had to be selfish about my own happiness and peace of mind. I refused to keep putting my own needs to the back and regretting those choices later in life. Tonight was the night that Robert was going to be all mine again and I was tingling with anticipation. I should have never ever left him for Justin anyway. That had to be the stupidest shit I have ever done along with trying to raise me and Robert's children as Justin's. As I thought back on all of it all I could say to myself was wow. What was keeping Robert? I wondered to myself. I figured he would have been here by now. Damn I hope he didn't see Justin's funky one leg ass and get mad at me again. I had to come clean with Robert once and for all. Fuck all of the bullshit this is the rest of my life we are talking about here. I called his phone but he didn't pick up. I left him a voice message and I texted him as well. I just wanted him to know that he was on my mind and that I couldn't wait to see him. I was startled out of my skin by the crashing of my front door getting bashed in. Justin came through the door carrying a gun aiming it at me.

Today has been a busy one and I was tired as hell, but I knew that I was going to see Kierra today so that thought gave me energy. I put my phone on the charger and went to take a hot shower. While in the shower my mind was filled with pornographic fantasies of what I wanted to do to Key. I thought to myself that she was getting this dick tonight. The head was fire no doubt but it was time for me to put this pressure up inside of her. My dick was so hard thinking about it all that I could have cut diamonds with my shaft. I masturbated in the shower just to take off the edge so I wouldn't be busting on Key in 3.0 seconds. I got out of the shower drying off and looking for the cologne that Key likes so much. I heard sirens going past outside and wondered what could be happening in this bougie ass neighborhood. Probably an elderly person has fallen or had an attack of some sort I figured. I continued getting ready for my rendezvous with Key smiling on the inside and the outside beaming with excitement.

I knew something was wrong even before I walked out my door to flashing lights around the corner at Kierra's place. She had called me and texted me but she didn't pick up when I tried to hit her back. An intense melancholy enveloped me and tears began to run from my eyes as I watched a covered body being pushed out of Kierra's condo by the paramedics. I began to run over to her place. I had to see what the fuck was going on. The area was taped off and cops and medics and firemen were milling about. One of the cops stopped me as I tried to go under the tape. "Sir this is a crime scene you cannot enter" he told me sternly. "This is my girl's place officer. What the hell is going on?" I asked him sharply. He looked at me and I could see his demeanor change. I began to weep. "A young lady was shot and killed in there sir. And the apparent assailant then turned the gun on himself. Both persons are deceased. I'm so sorry sir" he finished sadly.

I had apparently lost consciousness because I awoke in a hospital bed with IV's running from my arms. I thought back to what had happened and fresh tears filled my eyes. I looked around to see my mom and sister as well as Kierra's mom and sister. "Please tell me that I was having a nightmare. Please tell me that my baby is ok" I whimpered to the room. Kierra's mom ran out of the room crying and that was my answer. All I could do was lay there and wallow in my misery and despair. I wanted to die too, I couldn't eat or drink anything. I just wanted my life to be over so I could join Kierra in the afterlife. All of that changed when Kierra's mom and sister brought the kids to me and told me that they were my responsibility. The sadness in both of the children's eyes made me want to take away their pain. I have to man up and be a father to these two and the son that Beverly and I have. The next day I was released from the hospital, and I began the new life of being a single dad. I still mourned for my sweet Kierra and I enjoyed seeing her in our babies. Life must go on.

Printed in the United States
By Bookmasters